Dark Earth
Rising

Circus at Devil's Landing

Debra Castaneda

This is a work of fiction. Names, characters, places, and events either are the products of the author's imagination or are used fictitiously. Any resemblance to actual persons living or dead, events or locations is entirely coincidental.

ISBN: 979-8-9877469-4-3
Edited by: Lyndsey Smith, Horrorsmith Editing
Cover design by: James, GoOnWrite.com

For Tara, who said the beasts deserved an origin story.

Chapter 1

California
April 1906

Devil's Landing lay in ruins behind me. The shaking had been brief, but the devastation in the harbor and on land was complete. Fire began to consume several low buildings, their occupants running in panic toward the water.

As screams ripped through the air, piercing the chaos and confusion, I fled to the marsh.

Guilt fueled me as much as fear.

I'd been running for what felt like an hour but couldn't have been more than minutes, when I arrived at the slough.

Stumbling over the soggy, unfamiliar ground, I never dared to look back. The shouting and shrieking grew fainter. I hid in the tall damp grass, gasping for breath.

The mud seeped through the soles of my shoes, and the dampness of the early morning mist pressed down on me, like a shroud. The air reeked of rotting vegetation.

A noise nearby made me freeze. Someone was running on the path nearby.

I held my breath, desperate to remain hidden among the grasses.

Chapter 2

Las Peñas, Mexico
March 1906

"What are you going to do, señorita?"

With the sun rising into the blue sky ahead, we rode side by side on the widening trail. My thighs stung, raw from the long ride. The soothing morning air carried with it the chorus of birds and the steady rhythm of clopping hooves.

"I'm going to find the man who took Javier and buy him back," I said to Felix.

Ambrose Hinsworth was intimidating, but he was also a businessman running a successful circus, and my offer was generous. I just dreaded seeing the Englishman again. When my brother, Nestor, had brought him to the hacienda, he'd looked me over like I was something he wanted to devour.

"Was Javier a slave?" Felix asked, troubled.

I shook my head. "No. Of course not. Javier is paid to manage the fields." The truth was more complicated than that. My brother had broken with my father's tradition of paying the field workers in cash. Instead, Nestor made them work for food, clothes, shelter, and a small plot of land where they could grow whatever they liked. But secretly, I gave them pesos.

"Then how could your brother sell him to the circus man?" Felix persisted.

The town wasn't far off now. I urged the horse to trot.

"He had no right." My grip on the reins tightened.

"I saw Nestor kicking Javier before the circus man took him away," Felix admitted in a sly voice. At sixteen and with sharp eyes, the stable boy had guessed our secret.

My cheeks burned with the memory.

Felix must have heard Nestor that night. *"You whore!"* His drunken roar still rang in my ears.

I could feel the boy staring at me. Our journey together had emboldened him.

"Senorita," he began, "my sister says it's wrong for you to like Javier so much."

The idea of the laundress gossiping about me made my chest tighten. Yet she wasn't the only one to hold that opinion. Not even my father understood my feelings for Javier, but my father hadn't known all I'd been through. Javier was the only person who didn't recoil at the secret I hid from the world. He was the only man who could ever love me.

I couldn't ever lose that…or him.

So, I ignored the boy's insinuation. "What did señor Hinsworth do with Javier?"

Felix dipped his head. "I didn't see nothing, señorita. I was scared and hiding. Your brother was borracho and everything."

Nestor gave—or sold—six of our workers to Hinsworth. The ones he called troublemakers, who'd threatened to leave the hacienda. Nestor had gone to Las Peñas to deliver coffee beans to the ships docked at the port and returned with the circus man, then Javier and the others disappeared. What Hinsworth wanted with them, I did not know, but it could not be good.

When we arrived in Las Peñas, the plaza was already bustling with people. The sun sparkled on waves lapping against the rocky shoreline. Small fishing boats bobbed in the water, and pelicans soared across the azure sky. Of the many ships in the harbor, one was much larger than the others, with four masts. It was the only boat big enough to carry a circus.

"Señorita," Felix said, "the people. They're looking at you."

I'd been so lost in my thoughts—wondering how and where to start my search for Javier—I hadn't noticed. People were staring at me, most of them vendors lingering in the shade of lean-tos made from palm trees.

I sat astride my horse—a position reserved for men.

My exhausted legs wobbled like jelly when I dismounted.

At the far end of the plaza, closest to the water, was the peak of a red and white striped tent. Dread squeezed my chest.

"Find a place for the horses to rest. Stay with them until I return."

"How long will you be gone?" Felix's expression gave away his unease. He'd ridden alongside me for seventy miles without complaint. I didn't want to ignore the boy or put him in danger. But I had to find Javier.

"Not long, I hope." I dug back into a pocket and handed him some coins, nodding at a nearby food stall. "Get something to eat and drink, Felix. Don't talk to anyone, and whatever you do, stay away from the river. There are crocodiles there."

His enormous eyes grew wide. "It's not the crocodiles I'm afraid of, señorita. It's señor Hinsworth that scares me bad."

Unable to find words of reassurance, I hurried across the plaza.

Chapter 3

Halfway across the plaza, I heard the unmistakable deep voice of Ambrose Hinsworth. My pulse throbbed, and I battled the urge to confront him. It was too soon for that. I needed a disguise.

At a stall selling hats, I bought a sombrero and stuffed my long hair under it. To hide my breasts, I purchased a brown serape and draped it over my shoulders, the ends coming together over my chest.

When I rounded the corner, Hinsworth stood leaning against a wall, a cigar hanging from his lips, hair yellow in the sun. No sign of Javier. The Englishman looked around, tapping a foot and scowling, like he was waiting for someone.

Hooves clopped against the cobblestones. A caravan of donkeys approached, pulling carts with tarped cages. I could not see what the cages held, but the moans and wails coming from underneath the coverings told me what I needed to know.

People started to gather at the front of the caravan, and Hinsworth dashed forward, yelling at them to back off. His workers were too busy shooing away a group of children to pay attention to me, so I darted to the last cage, which was rocking slightly on its precarious perch.

Fingers wriggled through a gap. My eyes registered the ring made of red and yellow beads.

Madre mía de Dios.

"Javier," I hissed.

"Ana Maria! What are you doing here?" The words came out slow and slurred.

"Did they drug you?" Thick cords securing the cage and its tarp made it impossible to widen the opening any further.

"Yes. They made us drink it." He paused. "Nestor will beat you when he finds you."

I ran my hand over the skin on his wrist. It felt cold. "I'm not going back. We'll run away. I have money. I'll buy you back from Hinsworth."

"No!" Javier squeezed my hand. "Stay away from him, Ana Maria. Please. He's dangerous."

"Did he take you to work on the ship?"

"Maybe. I don't know."

The sound of a boot heel clacking on the cobblestones made me glance up. The donkey herder glared in my direction. I dipped my head so the sombrero covered my face and darted into the closest alley. When the wooden wheels began to rumble, I peered around the corner and watched the caravan move down the street. At a safe distance, I followed until they reached a jetty at the edge of the water.

One by one, the crates of human cargo were loaded onto small boats and transported to the large, masted ship.

Still wearing trousers, I waited several minutes before following Hinsworth into the dim bar. Just a few men stood at the counter. Hinsworth wasn't among them.

"Did a man with yellow hair come in here?" I asked the bartender, adjusting the serape over my dusty white blouse.

The bartender scowled. "No ladies."

I nodded toward a corner where several women sat sprawled, bosoms hanging out of their corsets. "What about them?"

The bartender threw his head back and laughed. "Those ain't ladies."

I reached into a pocket and slid a few coins across the counter. "Do you remember the yellow-haired man now?"

The bartender had a round, bald head and puffy lips. He sneered at the coins. "Not for *that* much."

I sighed and produced a bill.

He snatched it from my fingers. "He's in the back room."

More haggling produced a bottle of tequila and two glasses. As I'd learned in the family business, negotiations usually went smoother when liquor was involved. I grabbed the bottle and found Hinsworth in the back room, but he wasn't alone. A woman sat on his lap, his hands under her skirt. I cleared my throat. Both were so preoccupied, I had to stomp my foot to get their attention.

He stared at me blankly for a few moments, then his eyes snapped open in recognition. "Somehow, I don't think your brother would be too happy to see you this far from your ledgers, Miss Carillo." He pronounced it Cah-ree-low, and it made me want to smash the bottle against his head.

"I'm here to discuss some private business." My steady voice did not betray the nervousness I felt inside.

Hinsworth pushed the woman off his lap. When she remained by his side, hand caressing his neck, he slapped her behind and gave her a little push toward the door. "I'll find you later, darling." Turning his attention to me, he took in my outfit and raised his eyebrows. "Did you ride all the way from San Sebastián? Lucky horse."

Instead of answering, I poured tequila into the two glasses and took a seat across from him. I drank mine down. Hinsworth tipped back his chair, staring at me with an amused, expectant expression. He had pale, rough skin and deep-set gray eyes. Not a handsome man, but striking. Dust covered his finely made clothes.

"You don't look anything like your brother," he said, picking up his glass.

No. No, I did not. Nestor was short, with a round face and barrel chest. I was taller, with a heart-shaped face, like my mother.

"You took Javier," I said. "We need him on the farm. He manages the fields and the workers."

Hinsworth gave me a sharp look. "I thought that's what your brother did."

"Nestor is a drunk," I snapped.

The circus man's lips twisted into a cold smile. "Maybe so, but your coffee farm is no business of mine."

"Well, it is mine," I replied hotly. "We need Javier. I'll pay you money. Good money."

Hinsworth gave a little shrug. "I don't know what you're talking about, sweetheart. I don't have your lover. I was there, remember, when your brother found you two together. Naughty, naughty, and him nothing but a peon. Nestor was very upset about the whole thing. Javier is probably just laying low until things calm down. I certainly don't have him."

I shot to my feet, face burning. "Mentiras!"

Hinsworth made a clucking noise. "English, dove. I don't speak your language."

"The cages," I sputtered. "I saw them. You have Javier!"

"I don't." Hinsworth slowly rose from his chair, shaking his head, and I stepped back. He was a tall man. Cocking his head to the side, he rubbed his thigh. "Now, I'd be willing to pay you good money if you were inclined to show me some of that Mexican hospitality you bestowed on that peon. I think you'd find me much more…satisfactory."

"Pinche cabron," I muttered, then turned on my heel and left.

Hinsworth's hollow laughter followed me out of the room.

I winced and stiffened. My back itched like it did whenever I got angry. It felt like it was on fire.

Chapter 4

As the orange sun set over the water, I learned the *Iron Maiden,* carrying Ambrose Hinsworth's traveling circus, was due to sail in two days, destined for San Francisco. A line of men stood outside the red and white tent near the gangway.

"Some workers ran off when she docked," a man with a weathered face said, following my gaze. He was dressed in overalls and a tattered shirt. "They're trying to find new people to take their places."

I stared at the tent for a long time. Felix had disappeared, along with the horses. I didn't blame him. Nestor would beat him senseless if he returned. My attempt to buy Javier's freedom had failed. I needed to make a new plan.

The place I secured to stay the night was a small inn off the plaza. My bed was lumpy and the blankets itchy, but exhaustion quickly overwhelmed me. I drifted off to a fitful sleep filled with dark visions of Javier in a cage onboard the hulking, four-masted *Iron Maiden.*

The next morning after breakfast, I knew what I had to do. The idea had come to me, fully formed, in the darkest of my dreams.

I strode toward the red and white tent, wearing the best dress I'd brought to Las Peñas, a colorful sash tied around my waist.

A woman sat behind a rickety table just outside the entrance to the tent, talking to an older man, thick around the middle. After a few moments, his shoulders drooped, and he slunk away, muttering. I prayed Hinsworth wasn't around.

Pushing my shoulders back, I stepped toward the table. It was covered in thin, leather-bound books.

Accounting ledgers. The tools of my trade.

The woman looked up, eyebrows rising. Close to forty, I guessed, with a high-bridged nose, remarkable violet eyes, and a profusion of auburn hair.

"Well," she said, "you're the most interesting thing I've seen all day. How do you do? My name is Ewa. Fortune teller."

"Would you tell mine?" I asked.

The woman shook her head, earrings tinkling. "Not today. I'm hiring for the journey north. We need roustabouts and artists." She looked me over again. "Do you have any…special talents?"

"I can sew. Beautiful costumes." I spun around slowly. "I made this dress." With help from Javier's sister, who was famous for her sewing skills, but Ewa needn't know that.

The woman drummed long, pale fingers on the table. "We already have a seamstress. Can you walk a tightrope? Swing on a trapeze? Contort your body?"

My insides shriveled. I was not a performer.

But I did have something that made me special. Something a circus might appreciate. The idea filled me with revulsion, but I needed to get on that ship and find a way to free Javier.

"I do none of those things," I admitted. "But I do have something, if you will permit me to show you in the privacy of the tent?"

Ewa regarded me with shrewd eyes for a long moment, then rose with some difficulty. She walked with the aid of a cane but gave no explanation.

"I hope you're not wasting my time," she said over her shoulder, picking up the ledgers and pushing through the flap.

It took a few seconds for my eyes to adjust to the gloom. Two bearded men with muscular arms sat at a long table, heads bent over large sheets of paper. Ewa ordered them away. They looked surprised but left through the rear of the tent without protest.

She dropped the ledgers on the table. "Well? You've got my attention. What can you do?"

My mouth went dry. Loosening the drawstring at the front of my dress, I allowed it to slip down to my waist. I removed my corset and chemise, dropping them on the table and resisting the urge to cover my breasts. After spreading my arms wide for the best effect, I slowly turned around, my face burning with my immodest display. I had never shown my body to anyone but Javier before, and it was for his sake I was doing it now.

Behind me, I heard Ewa gasp. "Oh my goodness. Never have I ever. Does it hurt?"

"Not anymore."

"But the shape!" Ewa cried. "It is…remarkable. Tell me, were you born with it?"

A sigh escaped my lips. "No."

"Fire?" Ewa guessed.

"Yes."

"An accident?"

"Yes," I lied.

"Impossible," Ewa hissed. "It's the evil eye."

El ojo de mal. The foreign clients of our coffee business were familiar with the evil eye. Surely, anywhere the circus might go, people would understand the dark meaning behind the shape on my back.

Behind me came the soft, rhythmic thumping of Ewa's cane against the dirt floor, and then the fortune teller was standing before me.

"That scar is interesting, but you can't expect people to pay good money to watch you stand there and do nothing," she said with a sniff of indignation. "People want to be entertained. You need to give them a performance, to entrance them."

My heart sank. Ewa was right, of course. I pulled up my dress.

"Do you have music?"

Ewa gave a dismissive snort. "We're a circus. Of course, we have music. The musicians are probably getting drunk somewhere in town. Why do you ask such a ridiculous question?"

Despite the fortune teller's abrupt tone, I could hear her barely disguised eagerness.

"Imagine music, then," I said in a hushed, dramatic tone. "Beautiful, mysterious music."

I lowered my head so my dark hair obscured my eyes. Slowly raising my hands in the air, I twirled around, my back once again facing Ewa. Arms undulating, I swung my hips to the right and up, twisting in a circle as I went. I lowered my hands to my shoulders and inched my dress down as I turned, gradually exposing the evil branding on my back.

Ewa clapped enthusiastically. "I can see how that might work. I saw a striptease in Paris. I can show you."

I spun around so fast I felt dizzy. "A striptease!"

Ewa scowled. "Now, don't get all ladylike all of a sudden, not when you were just dancing like Solome herself. We'll make sure your bubbies are covered. We're a family circus, so we'll show enough of you to entertain the men without offending the ladies." She paused, rapping her cane against the tent pole. "I wish Mr. Hinsworth could see you, but he left me in charge today, so consider yourself hired."

My relief was so great, my legs went weak. "Gracias."

Clapping from the far side of the tent made us both jump. A small man in a dark suit emerged from the gloom. "Hinsworth is going to love this," he said dryly. "But Ewa, have you forgotten something in your haste to hire this beauty? What *else* can she do?"

At first, I blushed. How long had this strange man been in the tent?

Then I couldn't help but stare. His face and neck were entirely covered in hair—his nose the most disturbing aspect. The hair was longest there and trailed down to his top lip. There was no hiding the sharp intelligence in his eyes. He resembled a lion. Or a dog.

Ewa rubbed the side of her face. "We'll think of something. I'm sure she has a skill."

"Besides spreading her legs? There's enough of that already. It's hardly fair to the rest of us, having to do two jobs to earn our keep." The hairy man turned to me and lifted his chin in a regal pose. "My name is Jacopo, the Lion Lord and assistant ringmaster."

"I can sew costumes," I repeated for his benefit.

"We have a seamstress," Ewa and Jacopo said in unison.

Remembering the ledgers, I offered, "I am good with numbers. And managing money. It's something I did for my family business. I can help with the accounting."

"You are familiar with the principals of accounting?" Jacopo's voice was laced with skepticism.

"More than familiar," I snapped. "I excel at it."

"Oh, she's humble too." He followed it with an amused little laugh.

Ewa cleared her throat. "Where did you learn English?"

"Finishing school," I lied. I'd had private tutoring, but my father never allowed me to leave the hacienda for a classroom. An American associate of my father's, who stayed with us when he visited San Sebastián, had taught me English.

"Oh, how fancy," Jacopo drawled. "Miss Finishing School might not want the job once she learns what it pays."

I didn't care about the salary, not if the job brought me closer to Javier. But I had to pretend if I didn't want to arouse their suspicion.

After we negotiated the salary—an abysmal sum—the fortune teller said, "The truth is, I can use some help with the books. I told Mr. Hinsworth my specialty is numerology, not accounting, but he's got even less of a head for it than I do."

"HB was desperate," Jacopo explained conspiratorially. "The manager quit at our last port."

"He and HB didn't see eye to eye," Ewa said hurriedly.

Jacopo snorted. "That's putting it mildly."

Ewa waved her cane in my direction. "I have people to hire, so go. Be at the dock no later than noon. If you're not here, we're leaving without you."

Panic bloomed in my chest. What would Ambrose Hinsworth say when he saw me? He'd know I was up to something, and he'd order me off the ship. I'd have to avoid him for as long as I could.

Ewa followed me out of the tent. When we were alone, her voice softened. "Don't forget to bring your own rags, dear, even if it's not near your time. There's something about being on a ship that can cause it to come early. You'll also need to supply your own towels, soap, and such. And bring a nice warm blanket."

"They don't provide those things on the ship?" I asked in surprise.

The fortune teller barked out a harsh laugh. "It's a boat, not a fine hotel. It's cold on the ocean and in San Francisco. If you have a good coat, you should bring it."

I had plenty of money in the silk pouch strapped to my thigh, so I hurried off to make my purchases.

Chapter 5

The footsteps slowed to a stop, replaced by heavy, raspy breathing.

I had no weapon and no place to run. My screams would be lost among those of the women and the shouts of the men. I tried to control my rising distress, knowing fear would only make me more vulnerable.

The footsteps resumed, eventually fading with distance, and I exhaled quietly. My body trembled, and my clothes were soaked and muddy, but I was safe.

Yet I still had the sense someone was nearby. The path was quiet and the slough still, but the feeling persisted.

I wasn't alone. Something was out there…in the shallows.

Madre mía de Dios. Don't let it be them.

On hands and knees, I crawled to a tree, wrapped my arms around its trunk, and peered at the stretch of water where the mist was thickest.

And then I heard it.

A splash, followed by a low growl. I knew that terrible, throaty noise all too well.

The brackish water began to writhe and churn as if something were stirring beneath its murky surface.

Could they swim? These things did not come from the sea.

My temples throbbed, and an icy chill rippled down my spine. I eyed the liquid blackness.

And then I remembered the accident, a whimper escaping my lips.

Of course, they could swim. I'd made a mistake fleeing to the slough.

Chapter 6

The sunlight didn't reach the lower decks to which I was confined. While my fellow travelers were busy settling in, I roamed the passageways, looking for Javier and the other men captured by Ambrose Hinsworth. My search ended abruptly when a green-eyed sailor discovered me.

"Are you lost, Miss?" He was a well-muscled man around my age.

"Just exploring," I lied. "I've never been on a ship before."

"It's best to stay in your quarters, Miss." He had an accent I didn't recognize, but it sounded nice to my ears. "The captain's strict about such things." The sailor paused for a moment, his eyes flicking over me, curious. "You're new with the circus, then?"

My eyes slid past him to the skinny stairwell, half expecting Hinsworth to appear.

"Yes," I said.

The passage was so tight, we were forced to stand inches apart. The man smelled of saltwater and sweat.

"Where did they put the cages? Señor Hinsworth has been very busy, and I thought I could check on them for him."

The man frowned. "They'll be far below, Miss, but the captain said no one is allowed near them, except for Mr. Hinsworth himself."

It was my turn to frown. "Have they had fresh water? Food?" The words came out haughtier than I intended, and the sailor rubbed the side of his face.

He leaned toward me, lowering his voice. "Have you seen them? Are they…fearsome?"

"Fearsome?" My fists clenched as I thought of Javier trapped in a cage. "Is that what you were told?"

He nodded solemnly. "Yes. They're dangerous animals. Captured in the mountains. That's why we stopped in Las Peñas—so Mr. Hinsworth could hunt them. He plans to show them in San Francisco, but first, he must train them."

My stomach heaved. Hinsworth planned to train them like animals! Surely, when the audience saw such an act, they'd leap to their feet and cry out in protest. Was Hinsworth mad? Did Ewa and Jacopo know? And what of the members of the circus who were still strangers to me? I would need to proceed carefully.

Caution was also required with this sailor. He could easily report me to his captain.

"Well, I understand that señor Hinsworth is a very talented trainer, and if anyone can do it, he can." The words nearly stuck in my throat, but misdirection was required.

He blinked, seeming not to know what to say.

I smiled. "Allow me to introduce myself. I'm Ana Maria Carillo."

He smiled back, showing good, clean teeth. It was like the sun coming out in that dark passage. "My name is Liam. I joined up in Liverpool, but I'm from Ireland. Never been to Mexico before, or California." He stepped away and stuck his head into the stairwell. A moment later, he said, "From what I've seen of Mr. Hinsworth, Miss, I'd take care. Avoid him, like. He's a bit of a goat."

And with that warning, the sailor scrambled up the steps and was gone.

Ewa lifted her arched eyebrows when I hurried in. "And where have *you* been?"

"Exploring the ship," I said casually, setting down my valise and looking around the room. It had a low ceiling and a long trestle table at one end, chairs on either side. There were shelves for storage but not much else. It was a spare room, hardly furnished.

"Where do we sleep?" I asked, mystified.

Ewa gave a rough laugh and limped to the far wall. "On these bunks, my dear."

I stared at the shelves. There were three long planks, each divided into two sections and attached with iron bars. A thin, dirty mat topped each one.

And then I understood.

They weren't meant for storage; they were for sleeping.

"Those aren't beds," I protested.

"While we're on the *Iron Maiden,* they certainly are." Ewa laughed, swinging her case onto a low berth. She tapped her cane against one of the top bunks. "You can sleep up there. The others are already spoken for."

"But…"

"No buts, my dear. These are the sleeping arrangements, such as they are, and there's no use complaining about it."

With a sigh of resignation, I picked up the tied-up bundle of necessities I'd bought in Las Peñas. "Where shall I put my things?"

Ewa gestured around the room with her cane, laughing again. "Do you see any wardrobes in here? You keep your baggage—and all the rest of your belongings—in your berth."

I climbed up to the top berth. There was barely enough room for me, let alone my belongings, and the mat was so dirty I could not bring myself to lay on it. My serape was large enough to cover the padding, so I'd use that as a sheet. With no pillow, a rolled-up coat would have to do. I stretched out. The wooden slats of the ceiling were less than two feet from my face. The berth was some two feet wide.

If I rolled over in my sleep, I'd fall to the floor and break something. I would have to take care.

Ewa directed me to the lady's washroom, which was in a shocking state. Lukewarm water trickled into a single stained washbasin, and the floors were damp and dirty. Lacking proper ventilation, the rooms stank, so I rushed through my business and scurried back to my quarters.

Jacopo, Ewa, and a stout woman sat at the table now piled high with colorful fabric. The woman had dull brown hair and bright round eyes, like a bird. She was sewing but looked up when I entered. Her smile revealed a wide gap in her teeth, which was very charming.

"Now, ain't she a pretty thing," she said.

Ewa was taking things from a box: pots of paint, brushes, and squares of stiff paper. The fortune teller was making her own tarot cards. Ewa was a talented artist. The symbols she painted were simply but beautifully done.

"The trick is, Ruth," Ewa began, "we need to find a way to show off what's on our señorita's back without her bubbies hanging out."

"Have you talked to HB about our newest member?" Jacopo asked, stroking his furry chin.

Ewa squinted at a half-finished tarot card. "HB's been too busy, hasn't he?" she finally said. "Talking with the captain and…other things."

"Yes, those other things! I can't wait to see them myself," Ruth added eagerly.

Ewa thumped the table. "Ruth!"

Ruth's face crumpled. "I'm sorry, Ewa. I shouldn't have said. I shouldn't have."

Jacopo patted her arm. "It's all right, Ruthie. We all want to see them. But they're not ready yet. That's what HB said, didn't he Ewa?"

Ewa pushed a finger between her eyes as they rolled upward. "What HB said is that we were to mind our own business until he finishes his."

"Who's this HB you're talking about?" I asked.

"It's our little nickname for Mr. Hinsworth," Ruth piped up.

Ewa sensed my confusion. "It's a private joke among the artists. It stands for 'horrible bastard'."

Jacopo shot her a look, then turned to me. "And you can keep that to yourself."

"Never mind all that," Ewa snapped. "We need to decide on your costume. Get that all sorted before I present you to HB. Jacopo's going to help you with your dance." She sniffed. "He's seen every striptease in Europe."

The Lion Lord shot to his feet and bowed. "At your service, señorita. You and I will choreograph a beautiful dance that will captivate the audience and make HB want to bed you."

Ruth giggled, then clapped a hand over her mouth. My insides twisted, and I glared at the small, furry man.

"That is *not* my intention," I said coldly.

"I didn't say it was." Jacopo's eyes twinkled with mischief.

Ewa sighed. "Don't mind him. He fancies himself a provocateur. Now, Ruth, about señorita Carillo's dress…"

Ruth hopped down from her chair and circled me, hands on her hips. "She's a tall one," she said over her shoulder. "And would you look at that tiny waist…and those curves. We'll want to accentuate those." She snatched up a length of fabric and held it against my skin. "This would do well with that dark hair of hers and her coloring."

I stared at the cloth against my arm. "It's almost the same color I am."

Ewa smiled. "That's the point."

I clenched my fists and took a deep breath. "But…"

"It will make you appear naked," Jacopo said.

I had imagined a costume of emerald satin, or a brilliant red, but even *I* could see the chosen fabric was a clever trick.

Ruth took my measurements, then sat at the table, biting her lip as she drew a quick sketch and held it toward us for inspection.

Ewa glanced up, nodded, and said, "Now isn't that clever." She turned to Jacopo. "Well?"

He sniffed and made a big show of considering the sketch. "It is genius."

No one asked my opinion, and I did not give it, mostly because I was still thinking about Hinsworth finishing his business below decks. Business that involved Javier. I had to find him and the others and free them. But how, and when? Even if I managed it, there weren't enough captives to overpower the crew. Timing would be everything. My opportunity would come the next time the cages were moved.

These thoughts were interrupted by the noisy arrival of more women. Jacopo introduced Louella and Clara, two sisters who did pantomimes—a comedy and music show to entertain the families. The young women eyed me suspiciously through heavy makeup. Their glances were not lost on Jacopo.

He leaned toward me and whispered, "They're worried you're a bit of competition for HB's attention."

"They needn't be," I muttered.

A beautiful woman with black skin and a regal air followed. Ewa introduced her as Miss Ofelia, goddess of the iron jaw. She sat next to Ewa and watched, entranced, as the fortune teller finished painting a heart with wings.

Three other women, nearly identical in appearance, formed a trapeze act called the Kastbar Sisters. Each had a tiny waist and cascading blond hair. If it were not for their bosoms, it would be easy to mistake them for children. They came from Germany and had joined the circus after running away from the drudgery of the family farm. Their names were Frieda, Gertie, and Herta.

After a simple meal of meat, potatoes, pickles, and hard crackers, we spent the rest of the evening in our quarters. Frieda tried to engage me in conversation, but when the women began asking questions about my life and why I'd joined the circus, I pretended to have a headache and moved my chair away from the group.

"She's got her nose up in the air," Gertie said, loudly enough to make sure I heard.

"She shouldn't," Herta replied. "Not with the way she talks. I can hardly understand what she says."

"Shush!" Frieda cried, casting a stricken look in my direction.

I ignored them, just as I'd ignored the women back home who'd gossiped about me, right in front of my face, at dinner parties in San Sebastián.

I'd not thought of bringing a book to pass the long hours, but Jacopo loaned me one—a novel written by an

Englishwoman named Jane Austen. The story of Anne Elliot temporarily distracted me from my worries as I read by candlelight, and the next few hours passed quickly enough.

But the novel could not distract me from the whispering that began at the far end of the table.

Did you see them? The cages?

Wild beasts. One of the sailors saw them.

HB won't let them loose around us, will he?

As exhausted as I was by the long day, sleep still eluded me. I hadn't shared a room since visiting my cousins a few years ago. In the morning, when they saw my scar, my cousins had refused to let me back in their room, saying everyone knew the mark on my back would cause death to anyone who looked upon it.

Lying on my bunk, I was aware of every sound, every breath, every whisper. Our quarters on the ship were too small for so many women.

Dread of meeting Hinsworth pressed down on me, as did the low ceiling. The ship was noisy. It seemed the sailors slept in shifts, so there was always a crew on the deck above, feet pounding, shouts shattering the night.

Eventually, I must have drifted off, only to be awakened by a distant wail.

I sat up so abruptly, I banged my head on the beams. Ignoring the lump forming on my forehead, I gripped the sides of my bunk, listening.

There it was again. I had not imagined it.

A low, mournful wail. Another soon joined it, and another, until it was a chorus of nightmares. To my astonishment, the others slept on. The Kastbar Sisters snored loudly, as did Ewa below me. They did not even stir.

I clambered down as quietly as I could, the iron-sheeted floor cold against my bare feet. Tiptoeing down the passage, I waited, holding my breath. Footsteps thundered overhead, then the unmistakable rumbled cursing of Ambrose Hinsworth. He was coming down the stairs. I looked around wildly. My room was at the other end of the long, narrow hall. He'd reach the landing before I could get there.

I dashed toward the lavatory and darted inside, just as Hinsworth slammed the wall with a fist, shouting, "Shut up, damn you!" His footsteps continued down the passageway.

When I was sure he had gone, I emerged. And then, a few moments later, another command from Hinsworth, this time directed at the men on the deck below.

"Get back to your rooms and stay there!"

Fear turned my blood to ice, and I thought about Javier and his companions confined to cages, an enraged Hinsworth heading toward them. More angry shouts. Anguished cries. And then silence. I leaned against a wall, my heart nearly exploding in my chest, my back twitching and burning.

A voice came from the stairwell. "Miss?"

I started violently, spinning around. It was Liam.

"Go back to bed, Miss Carillo. He'll be back soon. He's been drinking, and he has a whip."

Another round of tormented cries erupted from the depths of the ship, but this time, they were screams of pain.

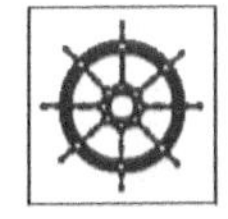

Chapter 7

I awoke to a rolling motion and the sound of retching. At first, I could not understand what was happening, but then I remembered—I was aboard the *Iron Maiden.* I peered over the side of my bunk. Ewa's auburn head leaned over a bucket, sick stretched across the floor. Frieda and Gertie were picking their way to the door, nightgowns covered in streaks of brown, towels clutched under their arms. Ruth, the seamstress, huddled in a corner, heaving.

I'd left my shoes on the floor next to Ewa's boots, and both were covered in curdled chunks. A foul, sour stench filled my nostrils.

"Go and get some buckets," Ewa gasped.

I grabbed my boots from the valise, shoved them on my feet, then made my way across the floor, taking care where I stepped. The seasickness tormenting my companions did not trouble me, although the rancid odor brought bile to my mouth.

There was no time to stop in the washroom and tidy my hair. It was a good thing I'd fallen asleep in my clothes; I was presentable enough for the top deck.

The first person I spotted was Liam, halfway up a rope ladder, silhouetted against the blue sky. While the sea was rough, it wasn't due to a storm, only wind. The sails fluttered and snapped in the stiff breeze. The fresh air felt good on my face, and I breathed it in, clearing the stink from my nose.

The crew was too busy to notice me. I hovered near the door from which I emerged, careful not to get in their way, lest I be trampled. Chickens, pigs, and a dog ran about the deck. Several empty buckets had been stashed against a pile of rope, and I headed toward them, when two hands seized my shoulders and spun me around.

It was Ambrose Hinsworth, his face white with surprise. Or anger.

"What are you doing here?" he demanded, eyes blazing.

Pushing back my shoulders, I managed to keep my composure. "I joined your circus, señor Hinsworth. In Las Peñas."

He gave me a little shake. "But why? Why would you do such a thing?" There were dark circles under his eyes.

I opened my mouth to answer, when he shook me again, harder.

"You can't fool me, Miss Carillo. You're looking for that peon who abandoned you. I told you, I don't have him." His eyes traveled down to my bosom, then back up to meet my gaze. "You are of no use to me or my circus. We will leave you at our next port."

I lifted my chin, the lie easily forming on my lips. "You are right about one thing, señor Hinsworth. I was abandoned by the man I loved. He left for his village, and he is not coming back. But you are wrong about something too. I *am* of use to your circus. You can ask Ewa."

Without another word, he released my shoulders and stepped back, folding his arms across his chest. "Is that right?" he drawled.

"Yes," I replied stiffly. "That is right."

He still looked unhappy, but his eyes had lost the sharp edge of suspicion. "Why didn't Ewa consult me about this?" And then he stormed off.

I snatched up the pails and turned toward the passageway. The metal buckets clinked together. When I glanced down at my hands, they were shaking.

Night came, and the crew divided between working the sails and drinking. It was time to find Javier.

Six men emerged from the galley in front of me. They carried buckets of what appeared to be food and water, which sloshed over the sides. My heart began to race.

"Are you feeding the animals?" I asked, following them to the hatch. It sickened me to use that word.

A young man with a pointy chin and close-together eyes smirked. "If you want to call them that."

I pretended not to understand. "I thought señor Hinsworth had animals in cages below."

"Animals? Then you thought wrong," the young man said.

The others shook their heads and frowned. "You'd better shut your gob, Johnny," one warned.

The group vanished through the hatch. I stood in the fading light, trying to catch my breath. At least Javier and the others weren't starving.

But the knowledge offered little solace as dread clawed its way up my throat. I turned and went back to my quarters.

Chapter 8

A round head emerged from the water, and two yellow eyes stared at me. I crawled away as quickly as I could, slipping and sliding on the muddy ground.

The creature lunged forward, hissing and baring its teeth, and I clambered to my feet. Its face went slack.

For a moment, with a pain that seared my heart, our eyes met. Were those wild globes filled with rage and confusion the same that had once been gentle and kind? The creature seemed frozen with bewilderment. And, I hoped, also with recognition.

Hot tears clouded my vision, and I backed away. The beast slowly raised a clawed hand. In greeting? Or as prelude to an attack?

It began to growl, and I knew the answer. How foolish to think I might have a bond with such a monster.

I ran, darting between trees, leaping over fallen branches and dodging stumps, trampling the ragged hem of my nightgown as I went. My labored breathing was all I could hear.

Had it chased me? Every instinct told me to keep going, but I had to look. I turned around just in time to watch the creature slip back into the shadows of the marsh with a small splash.

But that's not all I could see in the early morning light.

The creature wasn't alone. The others were there too, heads bobbing just above the surface of the water. I could feel the bitterness in their fierce eyes.

Chapter 9

Before dawn, the rough, rolling waves returned. I couldn't sleep, so I escaped to the top deck and walked to the side of the ship. The wind unpinned my long hair. I shivered, wishing I'd worn my serape. Despite the cold, the sky was clear and the deepest blue.

A hand squeezed the back of my neck. I pushed it away and spun around.

It was Hinsworth, his mouth twisted into a sneer.

"Ana." The way he said my name sounded like a threat.

"Ana Maria," I corrected.

I rubbed the back of my neck where he'd touched it, as if I could brush away the taint.

"Ewa said you've quite a little gem to show me, Ana *Maree-ah*."

"In due time." I turned to leave. "I should check on Ewa and the others. They are not well."

He grabbed my arm. "I'm not a patient man."

I stared down at his hand. It was large, with long, strong fingers. A wave of panic numbed my wits.

Unable to think of a response, I sputtered. "Later…I…"

His eyes flashed, and then Hinsworth began to drag me across the deck. When I resisted, he swung an arm around my waist and began to half carry me. The tips of my boots scraped the deck, and I looked around wildly, trying to catch the eye of a sailor who might save me from whatever Hinsworth intended. They looked away and scattered.

I spotted Liam scrambling down a mast, but instead of hurrying toward us, he was running away. His betrayal pierced my chest like an arrow.

The ship's dog was alongside us now, barking in alarm. Hinsworth gave it a kick, and it yelped. Fury bubbled up at his cowardly, cruel act, my scar beginning to tingle, and I dug my nails into his arm. He pulled roughly at my hand.

Boots pounded the deck behind us.

"Ambrose," called a voice.

Hinsworth froze. It was Captain Pendergrast, with Liam standing behind him, panting.

"I've been looking for you," the captain said, acting as if I were not there. "I've just opened a bottle of port and thought you might like to join me."

Hinsworth tightened the grip on my arm. "It's a bit early for that." His voice was tinged with suspicion.

Captain Pendergrast shrugged. "A bit. But it's a hair-of-the-dog morning."

The captain turned on his heel, motioning for Hinsworth to follow. The circus owner rubbed his hand where half-moon crescents marked his skin. He shot me a look that promised he'd finish his business later. When they were gone, my knees wobbled with relief.

"You all right, Miss?" Liam asked.

"No," I said. "But thank you for bringing the captain."

Liam hung his head. "I should have done something myself, but he only listens to the captain."

His green eyes avoided mine, and I felt sorry for him. His position on the crew was a lowly one, and if he'd dared to confront an important paying passenger, he would have risked his job—and probably a beating by Hinsworth.

"You did do something," I reassured him. "The smartest thing you could."

His face relaxed, and a hint of a smile came to his lips.

Despondency overcame me. To avoid Hinsworth, I had to stay confined to my gloomy quarters. I'd had no luck sneaking below deck to find Javier and let him know I was aboard, working on a scheme to free him and the others.

But *what* scheme? And with *whose* help? Whom could I trust? Frieda, perhaps. Not Captain Pendergrast. The cages were paid cargo, and it was unlikely the captain would do anything to jeopardize his fee, no matter how unsavory the goods.

And what about Ewa and Jacopo? How much did they know about what was in the cages? Hinsworth struck me as a man who could keep his secrets, even from his own employees, if it served him. But the fortune teller and the Lion Lord were shrewd enough to guess and smart enough to keep their suspicions to themselves.

I paced the room along the length of the table until Ewa waved her hand at me from her berth, where she lay with a wet towel over her forehead. "Ana Maria, please. Spare us your clomping about."

Too restless to sit and read, I retreated to the passageway.

From somewhere, a bell rang, announcing lunch. The sailors stayed above at mealtimes, so this was my best chance at avoiding detection.

I descended a level cautiously. All was quiet. Then a door flew open, and an enormous man stepped out, hand over his mouth. His skin had a sickly, greenish tint. By his muscular build, I guessed he was the strongman. Wearing only a loose shirt that brushed his knees, he lurched toward the lavatory, and moments later, I heard miserable retching.

The wooden stairs creaked beneath my feet as I tiptoed down to the lower deck, heart pounding in my chest. I made my way with as much stealth as I could manage, pressing my ear against several closed doors. They had to be storage rooms. There were no sounds, and I wondered if Javier and the others had been drugged or beaten until they were insensible.

The passageway narrowed, then ended at a heavy wooden door. It had an iron ring in the center, which I pulled. The door rattled but did not open—it was locked. None of the other doors had locks. Was this the room holding Javier?

I gave the door a light tap. "Hello?" I whispered.

Silence. I tried again, a little louder.

"Javier? Are you in there?"

And then I heard it.

Someone was crying. It didn't sound like Javier. The voice was too high and thin.

My tapping became more insistent. "Hello? Can you open the door? Can I help you?"

The cry became a wail of despair. "No one can help me."

In frustration, I pulled on the ring. My skills involved numbers in ledgers, not picking locks.

"Go away," said the voice, more afraid than annoyed.

I leaned my forehead against the door. "No. Not until you tell me why you're in there…and how I can help you."

"Who are you?" The voice quavered like a reed in the wind. Each word seemed to require great effort.

"My name is Ana Maria Carillo. A passenger on the ship. Cómo se llamas?" In my nervous state, I'd slipped into Spanish, something I'd managed to avoid so far. "What's your name?" I repeated in English.

A long silence followed.

"Silas," he finally said.

"Why is the door locked, Silas?"

He gave a little moan. "You'd laugh if you saw me."

"No, no, no," I cried, keeping my voice low. "I would never laugh. At anyone. Who's keeping you down here like this? Tell me, por favor."

There was a scratching noise, like something dragging across the floor. "It doesn't matter," Silas replied. "Nothing matters. And you can't help me. I'm beyond help."

The despair in his voice brought a lump to my throat. "Do you know anything about the men in cages down here?" I asked, then held my breath.

More scraping across the floor. "I won't do it." Silas sounded close, just on the other side of the door.

"What do you mean? Do what?"

"Go away," he hissed.

"Not until you tell me what you mean."

"I'm already ruled by one master," Silas said, his voice muffled. "I won't be ruled by another."

He was talking in riddles. Perhaps he was mad. Silas sounded weak, but maybe on the other side of the door was a deranged and dangerous man. It certainly wasn't Javier. I backed away and stared at the door.

"Ana Maria?"

"Yes?"

"It was nice to have your company." His tone was formal, cautious. "Go away now, and don't come back."

A fist—or something like it—slammed against the door so hard it rattled, and I fled upstairs.

Chapter 10

From Liam, I learned the official cargo list included liquor and coffee destined for merchants in San Francisco. The coffee, of course, came from my family farm, and it appeared my brother was more devious than I'd imagined. Nestor had kept the size of the transaction a secret, which meant he'd pocketed the money, depriving our business—and me—of our share.

There was no mention of human cargo.

No mention of Silas.

When the sea finally calmed, Ewa, Jacopo, and the others emerged from their berths, as unsteady as newborn lambs. There was a long wait for the washrooms and many grumblings about the lack of warm water. Jacopo, with all his hair, had taken to the top deck, where sailors splashed him with buckets of water.

"You smell worse than a wet dog, mate." Johnny, one of the sailors, laughed.

It took Ewa and me forever to comb through his tangles and restore Jacopo's hair to its former Lion Lord glory. When we were done, the other women joined us on the top deck, and we set to washing our clothes, using rainwater collected in barrels.

I picked up a white blouse and scrubbed a stubborn stain. "Frieda," I began, keeping my voice low, "is there someone named Silas in the circus?"

Frieda went perfectly still. "Yes. He's got some disease, or something, so he's not allowed out anymore. Or that's what Ewa said. Then she told me to mind my own business."

"But who is he?" I persisted.

Frieda glanced around nervously. "HB's brother, I think."

A gasp escaped my lips. Was Hinsworth so cruel as to keep his ill brother locked in a room, unattended? I knew the answer. After all, Hinsworth had captured and enslaved men.

"Have you ever seen Silas?"

"No," Frieda said. "Not many people have. Ewa, for sure. She's been with HB from the beginning—back in Liverpool, where he started the circus."

"But how can you not have seen Silas?"

"It's the strangest thing," Frieda said with a shudder. "He gets moved around in a box with holes. Sometimes, we hear him crying. It's a wonder HB hasn't left him in a sanitorium."

I remembered what Silas said about being ruled by one master. He had to have meant his brother.

The deck was more crowded than I'd ever seen it. The men had come out to wash their clothes too, and the sailors were taking turns. Shirts, pants, blouses, and skirts fluttered in the wind.

Hinsworth sat on a chair on the upper deck, smoking a cigar, watching me all the while.

Frieda peered up at him. "HB has his eye on you."

I tossed the dirty water from my bucket over the side of the ship, wishing I could dispose of Hinsworth as easily. "I hadn't noticed."

"You'll want to take care." Frieda nudged my side with a sharp elbow. "Herta took up with him. I warned her, but she wouldn't listen. Got her heart broken."

I gave Frieda a hard stare, indignation burning in my veins. Did this woman really think me capable of falling for that vile man? I did not want her spreading rumors about me.

Her blue eyes widened. "Why are you looking at me like that? I'm just trying to help."

"I don't need your help."

Frieda blinked. "I didn't mean to offend you," she said stiffly. "You're new, and HB can be charming when it suits him."

Hinsworth rose, crossed to the railing, and stared down at me. I looked away. There were plenty of people around. Surely, he wouldn't try and drag me off again, not in full view of Captain Pendergrast.

The captain glanced up. He observed Hinsworth watching me and, with a frown coming to his face, shouted, "Hinsworth, bring me a cigar and join me, won't you?"

Hinsworth turned and went to the captain.

It was the chance I'd been hoping for. I snatched up my undergarments, went to the lower deck, and tossed the clothes into my berth.

Then I ventured below deck again.

On my way down the steep ladders, I encountered no one. In the narrow passageway opposite Silas's locked room, I picked my way across a maze of crates, the smell of raw coffee beans filling my nose. There was only one place left where Javier and the others could be kept: a room at the back of the ship. I moved toward it, and as I drew closer, I could see a key hanging from a hook.

It must have been there for whomever was tasked with delivering food and water to the captives.

Snatching the key with trembling fingers, I fit it into the lock. The rough wooden door swung open with a creaky groan.

I gasped at the sight before me.

Inside a single cage, six men huddled together, wearing just pants. Their skin was covered with bruises and lash marks, making my heart clench in my chest. The stench of their sweat and waste was overpowering.

The men looked at me, their eyes full of fear and desperation. I recognized them. Emiliano. Pablo. Rudolfo. Manuel. Jose.

Rage surged within me, and I pulled the door shut.

Javier stepped around them. He'd lost weight since I'd last seen him, his condition deteriorating in this room of cruelty, without light or fresh air.

His eyes widened, and his mouth dropped open. "Oh no," he cried. "What are you doing here, Ana Maria?"

Rushing to the cage, I said, "I got a job with the circus. I don't have time to explain, mi amor. Just trust me. When we get to San Francisco, I'll find a way to get you out, and then we'll run away."

Javier shook his head. "That cabron will kill you if he finds out."

The men stepped away to give us privacy. They averted their eyes and murmured among themselves.

Javier thrust his hands through the bars and seized mine, squeezing with a desperate intensity. His eyes glistened with tears. "I love you, Ana Maria." His voice was a sorrowful rasp. "I always have, but you can't save us. It's too late." His fingers were clammy and icy cold.

At home, fear of my brother came between us. Now, it was bars of iron.

"It's not too late!" I cried. "I'm here. I'll find a way, no matter what."

Javier let out a shuddering breath. "There's something on this ship. A very bad magic, Ana. I can feel it, and it's coming for us. Now go, please, before it gets here."

Javier's father was a curandero. If he said there was bad magic about, he would know. I believed him.

"Is it señor Hinsworth?" I asked.

Javier's shoulders drooped. I hated seeing him so worn out, the light gone from his beautiful dark eyes.

"I don't know," he whispered, his voice breaking. "Maybe. It's not like anything I understand." He stared down at my hand and stroked it. The ends of his fingers were calloused from hard work but still gentle and caressing.

Heavy footsteps sounded on the deck above.

Hinsworth.

Javier snapped his head up, resolution replacing fear in his dark eyes. "Go, Ana. Please go, before it's too late."

When I shook my head, he snatched his hands away, and the sudden loss of his touch made me dizzy.

"Ana, you have to go," he repeated. "For me. Now."

I hesitated, but then I saw his hand come to his chest. He patted his heart and pointed at me.

With a sob rising in my throat, I left.

Chapter 11

There was only one way in and out of the lower deck, and that was the ladder. Hinsworth would find me if I didn't hide. Panicked, I looked around and spotted a stack of crates next to the bulkhead, with just enough space for me to squeeze behind.

Hinsworth descended the ladder, and my heart raced. He headed away from my hiding spot, his boots thudding on the wooden planks. To Silas's room, then. There was a jangle of keys and the door creaking open, then a thin, high cry.

"Brother!" Hinsworth boomed.

"I said I won't do it." Silas's voice was defiant. Petulant.

"And I say you will."

Silas laughed, an empty, tinny sound.

The echoes of a struggle followed. Hinsworth grunting. A scuffle. Nails scraping against wood.

Hidden deep in the gloom, I peered out. Hinsworth emerged with something in his arms.

It was Silas. His head was small, his neck slender, his hair a cap of golden curls. He had no legs, just long thin arms with small pale hands.

Hinsworth carried Silas pressed against his hip, as a mother would carry a small child.

"I don't want to go," Silas whimpered.

"Isn't this what you're always going on about?" Hinsworth sneered. "Us back together again, like the old days?"

"It's too late for that," Silas cried. "Not after that butcher of a surgeon ruined my life."

Hinsworth scoffed. "It's not my fault there were only legs enough for one of us."

Madre mía de Dios.

I'd heard of such a thing before. In a small village near San Sebastián, twin girls had been born joined together at the middle of their bodies, with one set of legs between them.

Hinsworth and Silas had once been attached. A doctor, somewhere, had performed a miracle but created an inequity.

Silas buried his head in his brother's neck. Even though his voice was muffled, I heard him say, "I won't do it. I won't." And then a high-pitched screech. "You're hurting me. Stop!"

Hinsworth exhaled loudly. "Just this one time, Silas. For me. I promise."

Silas sniffed. "You said that before, and it was horrible. I told you it would be horrible, and it was."

"We didn't know as much back then, did we?" Hinsworth said, voice cajoling. "I need this. *We* need this. And you owe me, brother. After everything you've done."

Silas sighed in resignation. "All right."

"You can do this. I know you can."

Silas gave a small laugh, so cold it made me shudder.

"I know it too, brother. Now take me inside."

Hinsworth slowly carried Silas past the crates and my hiding place, into the room where Javier and the other captives were imprisoned.

When the door shut behind them, I escaped.

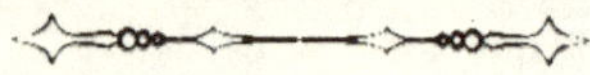

I returned to the women's quarters just as Ruth was finishing my costume. With a flourish, she picked it up from the table and shook it out, loose threads flying.

Still in a daze from what I'd witnessed below deck, I took the dress, went to the corner by my bunk, and put it on. I returned to the group, and to my surprise, everyone clapped. There was no mirror—I could not see myself. The fabric was thin and nearly the same color as my skin. The front was high, fastening around my neck. My arms were left bare, as was my entire back. The material flowed to my ankles.

"You look beautiful," Frieda exclaimed. "Doesn't she sisters?"

Hertie and Gerta exchanged looks, then rolled their eyes.

When Ruthie spun me around to check a seam, Frieda gave a little shriek. "Oh my goodness, what is that?"

One of the pantomime girls—Louella—crossed herself.

Jacopo, tipping back in a chair, filing his nails, looked up. "It's a scar. Surely, you've seen one before."

I cringed, imagining an entire audience having the same reaction. If I escaped with Javier before the first performance, I wouldn't have to go through with it.

"But why's it shaped like an eye?" Louella asked, as if I weren't in the room.

Jacopo wriggled his fingers in the air. "Oooo, it's the evil eye. Beware, or it will cast a spell on you."

Louella clapped a hand over her eyes. "Will it, Ewa? Will it? Can you do something to protect me against it?"

My face heated up, and my body shook with indignation. My scar was a reminder of what I'd endured and the strength it had taken me to survive it. It did not have any powers or carry any sort of curse. But I said nothing and bit my lip instead.

Superstitious beliefs had convinced my mother and aunts the mark on my back meant something sinister, yet I felt no darkness within me. Despite my reassurances, they'd refused to see past their own fears and treated me with a distant and wary respect.

Ewa's mouth fell open. She got to her feet as if in a daze. Jacopo also rose. They stared at each other and began to laugh.

I cleared my throat and stomped my foot at their mockery. "I don't see what's funny."

Ewa recovered first. "I'm sorry, Ana Maria. It's not you. Not at all. But Louella here has proved herself quite useful, for once. She doesn't know it, but she's just suggested a means for us to make a little extra money."

"I don't understand," I said stiffly.

Jacopo patted my arm. "You will."

Chapter 12

Shelter. And people. I needed to find both. The land around the water was dense with tall grasses and trees. I stopped, disoriented for a moment.

The marsh—and its savage inhabitants—was on my right. I needed to get away from the slough. When the brush thinned out, I reached a dirt path scarred with deep grooves made by horse-drawn carts.

A lone house loomed in the distance. My knees went weak with relief at the sight of it.

I stumbled forward.

It looked like a painting. A two-story house set on top of a hill.

Much of the white-painted wood had peeled away, and the porch was crooked. With frayed curtains hanging in the windows, the place had an abandoned air. A bird on a fencepost chirped and stared at me with round, curious eyes.

There wasn't another house in sight.

I resisted the urge to sit on the porch and cry. Instead, I forced myself to walk to the door and knock. When no one answered, I knocked louder.

"Oh, please be home!" I yelled.

The bird flew away.

And then I heard voices.

I ran around the side of the house, down the grassy slope, until I saw them. A group of people stood around a barn that had collapsed. It was old and made of wood so weathered it appeared gray in the morning light.

I ran toward them, shouting hello, but they were too busy trying to corral a herd of bleating goats.

Beyond them was the slough.

From where I stood on the hill, I could see what they couldn't—a dark figure crawling out of the water and creeping along the sandy shore. It was approaching a small boy, with a cap of red curly hair, holding a baby goat. His back was to the water as he struggled up the bank, carrying the wriggling animal.

I screamed. As loud as I could. My rush of words came out in a mixture of English and Spanish. "Cuidado! Watch out! Mira! Something is coming!"

The group of people turned and looked toward me. Three men and two women. I couldn't see their faces clearly, but they definitely seemed confused.

I began pointing wildly. "The water! Look at the water!"

But it was too late. The creeping figure reached the boy and dragged him toward the marsh. The child let go a high, thin shriek, and then he was gone.

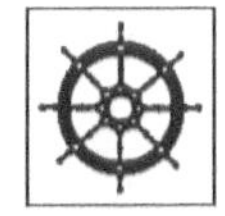

Chapter 13

After dinner, I escaped to the top deck, unable to endure the nervous glances and whispers. My scar had become a topic of conversation on a journey otherwise filled with idleness. There wasn't room on the ship for the troupe to practice their acts, so they entertained themselves the best they could. Those not inclined to read, sew, or draw gossiped, and I felt like an outsider among them.

They talked of things that meant nothing to me. I cared little for the circus or the attachments between performers, and I could not discuss my reasons for being on the ship. So, I adopted an amiable manner but kept my distance. Only Frieda tried to draw me in, but even she soon gave up.

As far as I could tell, Hinsworth was still below.

My chest tingled with dread at the wickedness he and his brother were inflicting upon Javier and the others. Two had wives and children back home. My brother had stripped them of their wages, then forced them to work. Though I paid them, nothing would convince them to stay at the hacienda and endure the terrible conditions my greedy brother had created.

I stared at the clouds scuttling across the graying sky.

Liam noticed me standing there and brought me a rough blanket to drape around my shoulders and a tall tin cup of milky black tea. He slipped a flask from a pocket and added a splash of whiskey. I smiled at him gratefully and took a cautious sip, feeling the liquid slide down my throat and warm my stomach.

Leaning against the railing, I looked out at the endless ocean, my thoughts turning once again to Javier.

Liam seemed uneasy. Finally, he cleared his throat. "Is it true what they say, Miss? That you have a mark of the evil eye?"

My throat went tight. Liam had been the first man to show me any kindness aboard the ship. He seemed different from the others, different from the people I knew back home.

"It's just a scar," I said, my voice low.

Liam nodded slowly, but doubt lingered in his eyes. "They're saying there's something...unusual about it."

It seemed rumors traveled just as fast on a ship as they did on the hacienda.

"Do they?" I said coldly.

Liam shrugged. "I don't believe it, Miss, but people are saying that anyone who looks on it will be cursed."

I clenched my jaw, anger rising within me. And guilt. After Nestor had left for Las Peñas, I'd gone to Javier's room. He had traced the raised flesh with a gentle finger. The next day, Hinsworth arrived and Javier disappeared.

Like he was cursed.

My blood ran cold.

My mother had warned my scar would bring bad luck. And it had.

"I won't keep you from your duties," I said.

Liam rubbed the side of his face. "I shouldn't have said anything, Miss. I'm sorry. I can see I've upset you. I thought they were just making things up."

It was my fault. I'd let down my guard with a stranger, and at the first opportunity, he'd betrayed me, choosing to believe in a silly superstition. Just as my own mother had.

Without another word, I set down the mug. Liam grabbed a handful of ropes, tying them off.

"We're in for a bit of rough weather tonight, Miss."

I squinted up at the nearly cloudless sky. "How do you know?"

"We had a red sunrise this morning." A grim smile stretched across his face. "Red sky at morning, sailor take warning."

I padded back to my quarters.

From across the room, Louella groaned. "How much longer are we going to be on this blasted ship?"

"Not much longer," Ewa said, rummaging through her valise. "A day, perhaps."

Louella groaned again. "I'll be dead by then, certainly. My time came early."

"It's the change in the weather that brought it on," Frieda said from her berth. "I've started mine too."

"And mine," added Frieda's sisters in unison.

Ewa sighed. "And here I was thinking I was the only one afflicted. We'll be a right mess when all is said and done. How about you, Ana Maria?"

I was shaking my head when I became aware of a heaviness in my lower belly. If I hadn't started, I was about to. Grabbing a pouch from my valise, I went to the lavatory and saw the blood. The hot water was gone. Only cold water dribbled from the tap. After cleaning up as best I could, I placed a length of flannel between my legs.

I was just walking into the room when I heard Louella say, "It's too early for mine to come. Something isn't right. It's Ana Maria and her evil eye that did it. Did it to us all."

"Oh, shush now," Frieda snapped.

"And if you don't, Louella, I'll give you a curse you won't soon forget," Ewa added.

"HB says you're just a fake," said Herta, Frieda's sister who'd taken up with Hinsworth.

"Did he now?" Ewa's voice was colder than any winter I'd yet experienced.

I was too restless thinking about Javier to read, and Ewa was in no mood to tolerate my pacing, so I climbed into my berth and stared at the flickering shadows on the ceiling. But the dancing light made my head hurt, so I closed my eyes and half listened to the women's complaints about the lack of water and not being able to properly clean their bloodied rags without it.

My stomach began to cramp, so I curled up and tried to sleep.

Exhaustion, pain, and worry crept over me, and I eventually drifted off, lulled by the rocking of the ship.

When I awoke, all the lanterns except for one had been extinguished. The ship rolled from side to side, more violently than before.

Somewhere below me, someone was moving around.

Probably one of the women trying to find her way to the door to use the lavatory.

Heavy breathing next to my berth jolted me to full awareness.

"Are you all right, Ewa?" I whispered.

The bunk quaked violently. Something was scaling the iron pole.

My skin prickled. A voice, ghastly and garbled, said my name. But it came out wrong. *Shanamara.*

Dread squeezed my chest. I pressed up against the wall, a scream rising in my throat.

From the shadows of the single lamp, a round dark head appeared near my feet. A misshapen face with a small malicious mouth filled with pointed teeth, its shoulders hunched and covered in matted, patchy fur. A creature.

With horror, I saw the ring made of red and yellow beads adorning one of its fingers. The ring Javier wore, made by his mother.

Madre mía de Dios.

What had Hinsworth done to him?

My throat convulsed, and then I screamed.

Chapter 14

The next thing I recall, I was sliding around on the wet floor, and people were yelling. I grabbed hold of the iron bar near our berth and managed to pull myself to a standing position.

"You gave us all a fright, with all that screaming fit to raise the dead," Ewa shouted above the cacophony of creaking wood and the roaring sea.

The storm Liam predicted had arrived. Waves had forced open the porthole, and water poured through it, drenching our beds and cascading to the floor. With Frieda's help, I pulled it shut. But before long, it banged open again. Defeated, we watched the water come in.

The other women huddled in their bunks.

I remembered the tortured, monstrous face that had appeared just before I'd lost consciousness and wondered if I had dreamed it.

A figure wearing an oilskin slicker appeared in the doorway, holding a lantern that swung back and forth. It was Liam, hair plastered to his face.

"The captain says the storm is only going to get worse," he yelled. "He wants you to go below and join the men."

"How long will this last?" Louella cried from the other side of the room.

Liam shook his head. "I don't know, but we haven't seen the worst of it yet."

Terror was etched on everyone's faces. We were all so vulnerable, at the mercy of the sea and the wind.

"Apúrate!" I cried, lapsing into Spanish. "We need to do what he says. Hurry up."

No one seemed enthusiastic about leaving their bunks, but when Ewa grabbed her cane, and then my arm, we all stumbled toward the door. Liam led the way, his lantern casting eerie shadows on the walls.

We descended the narrow ladder and staggered into the cramped men's quarters. Without a porthole, it was dry, but the smell of sweat and stale air filled my nostrils.

The men huddled around a table, playing cards. All except for Jacopo, who was retching into a bucket in the corner.

"What are you doing down here?" Strongman Jack asked gruffly.

"Captain's orders," Ewa snapped. "Make yourself useful, Jack, and fetch us some extra chairs."

One of the acrobats I'd yet to meet—a handsome man with dark curls—patted his bunk. "If any of the ladies would like to join me, I have plenty of room." He smirked. His berth was no larger than ours.

Herta said, "Don't mind if I do," and wobbled toward him.

Frieda leaned closer to me. "She'll bleed all over his bed, the state she's in."

Ewa stepped out of the room into the passageway, pulling me along with her. Some clever person had fixed iron rings to the walls, and we clung to those to keep from falling over as the floor rolled beneath our feet. Ewa's long auburn hair had come undone and hung in damp tendrils around her face.

"Something scared you up there. What was it?" she asked when we were alone.

I squeezed my eyes shut, trying to decide if I should tell her the truth. Even if I did, would she believe me? I could hardly believe it myself.

"I saw something. Something strange." My voice quivered at the memory. "A face."

Ewa's expression was calm. "Describe it."

When I finished, Ewa sighed.

"HB and some other men came looking for it. They clubbed it and dragged it away." She paused. "It's a good thing, too, because it would have given the girls a fright."

Her words hit me like a punch to the stomach.

"It!" I cried. "What you call 'it' is a man I've known since I was a child, and he has a name. Javier."

Ewa bit her lip, frowning and staring at me. After a moment, her brow lowered over her strange, violet eyes. "Is that why you wanted to join us? To find your man?"

"What else would compel me to leave my home?" I asked, my voice trembling with rage. "Ambrose Hinsworth took six men from my hacienda and put them in cages, like animals. I saw them myself below. And one of them was Javier."

Ewa shook her head. "Those aren't men. They're wild animals. Beasts. Strange and rare beasts."

I stared at her, unable to comprehend the enormity of her lies. "No. They are men, not beasts. If señor Hinsworth told you they were beasts, he was lying."

Jack had returned with chairs, and he stared at us as he lurched past. "What's going on?"

"Women's business," Ewa snapped, dismissing him with a wave. When he'd disappeared through the door, she returned her gaze to me. It was time to figure out what she knew.

"I discovered something else. Hinsworth has a brother he keeps locked up," I said. "His name is Silas, and he doesn't have any legs. He has to be carried."

Ewa's mouth fell open. "You saw him?"

"Yes."

She threw back her head and groaned. From seasickness, or despair, or maybe both. "Did HB take Silas anywhere near those cages with the…men?"

My body felt too heavy to move. All I could do was cling to the iron ring as the ship groaned around me. I nodded.

Louella stumbled past us, hands clutching her stomach. Even in the dim light, I could see she'd bled onto her skirt. She disappeared into the lavatory.

"I can't believe it," Ewa said, voice dull. Her eyes had a glassy look about them. "HB swore he'd stop. I should never have trusted him."

My thoughts returned to Javier. The last time I'd seen him, wearing only rags, he said he'd sensed dark magic aboard the ship. Javier had said his father was a curandero with the power to heal. My mother believed he was more than that. A brujo. A witch. Whatever powers the father had possessed, Javier swore he'd not inherited them. But he sometimes admitted he could feel things. Spirits. The presence of magic.

There was only one explanation, and I could hardly bring myself to say the words. "You think señor Hinsworth and his brother found a way to turn men into animals?"

Ewa's face was a mask, her eyes dark holes. The floor heaved beneath our feet, and we were thrown to the ground. Ewa crashed into a wall and slumped over. As I crawled toward her, I heard the frantic shouts of men from the top deck.

After Jack carried an unconscious Ewa to the men's quarters, I made my way to the top deck to see what was happening.

It was chaos. A bedlam of shouting. I clung to the door and peered out, moisture spraying my face. The shock of the cold water made me gasp. Each lurching movement of the ship shook my bones.

The boiling sea heaved around us. A fog-shrouded glow of red light pulsed in the distance, and we seemed to be making for it. A wave crashed over the side, sweeping a man off his feet. A net caught him before he could tumble into the depths, and it took two others to free him from the ropes. Minutes seemed like hours as I watched, helpless, while we careened through the storm.

There was a loud splintering sound, and the ship came to a violent, shuddering stop. Men went sprawling, and so did I.

The ship trembled and groaned, scraping across what must have been jagged rocks. Something struck my cheek, and I felt a stinging pain. When I managed to get my feet under me, I felt my face and encountered something sticking out of it. It was a splinter of wood. I pulled it out.

The roar of the raging ocean drowned my cries.

"We're taking on water!" a man shouted.

The frontmost mast began to tilt, slowly at first, then faster, tearing up pieces of deck as it fell.

Captain Pendergrast ordered lanterns to be tied to the surviving masts.

A whistle pierced the air.

Hinsworth was issuing commands of his own, and he led a group of sailors below deck.

Other men were frantically readying lifeboats. I went below and fetched everything I owned, slipping and sliding along the way.

When I reappeared, Liam was looking around, and when he saw me, he shouted, "There you are!" and pulled me toward a lifeboat.

Frieda and her sisters soon joined me, along with Louella, Clara, and Miss Ofelia. The Kastbar Sisters clung to each other, terrified. Just before the boat was lowered into the raging ocean, I saw Hinsworth appear, carrying a large box.

I knew what was inside.

Silas.

Two sailors rowed the lifeboat toward shore, the fog making it hard to see. The sound of waves crashing against the boat, accompanied by shouts and cries of panic echoing in the mist, assaulted my senses. More lifeboats dropped into the water, and the smell of brine permeated the night.

An enormous wave engulfed us. I pitched forward and would have been swept overboard if it weren't for Ofelia, who grabbed my skirt and held fast. When I'd pushed the hair out of my face and regained my breath, I noticed my valise was gone…and with it, my money. I cried out at the staggering loss.

We rocked back and forth in the wooden craft, and I imagined what would happen if we capsized, the taste of fear a bitter flavor on my lips.

It was only then that I remembered Javier and the others, left to their fate on the sinking *Iron Maiden.*

My belated concern was a stab to the heart. It was a cruel twist, to have followed Javier with the intention of buying his freedom, only to leave him behind to meet his death.

Chapter 15

The beasts had made it up the slough. I had to get away. There was nothing I could do for the family back at the farm, so I stayed on the dirt track, alert to every movement and sound. When I finally reached the harbor, chaos had turned to panic. Men gathered in groups around the mutilated bodies. Some of them held makeshift weapons, expressions grim and wary.

In the distance, my tent was still standing, so I hurried there, feet aching in my soggy shoes, hoping to find Ewa or Frieda.

The earthquake's destruction passed by in flashes. Parts of the wooden wharf had collapsed. Broken piers. More fallen warehouses. A bridge over the water buckled, railings tilted. People filled the streets, walking around with glazed eyes.

I was halfway to the tent when a deep voice bellowed, "Ana Maria."

With a blast of cold dread, I turned around.

Hinsworth was striding toward me, his face hard as stone.

"You can't run away from me, Ana Maria!" he thundered.

Chapter 16

I sat on the sand of a small beach, Frieda and her sisters a few feet away. We were too stunned to speak. Jacopo quietly talked with Ewa behind me, an arm around her shoulders. The circus troupe had made it safely ashore.

We were cold and miserable, but we were alive.

Fishermen soon came running and invited us to their cabins to dry out, promising something hot to drink and eat. But I refused to leave.

Ewa tried arguing with me. "You'll catch your death out here," she said, clutching Jacopo's arm. Ewa'd lost her cane in the tumult and seemed unsteady without it.

I shook my head. From the look on her face, she understood, and soon I was alone on the dark beach. Had the ship gone under before Javier and the others could be rescued? Would Hinsworth even try, or would he abandon them to a watery grave?

The salty brine of the ocean filled my nose as a lifeboat carrying Hinsworth appeared. A thick cloak of despair clung to my sodden clothes, like an invisible weight. I watched, too numb to do anything but huddle in the sand, shivering. He staggered through the rough surf, carrying the box containing his brother.

I wished they both had perished.

If Hinsworth noticed me, he gave no sign of it.

Several men bolted past and struggled through the surf until they reached the circus owner, who shoved the crate at them, then collapsed onto all fours in a heap of exhaustion. The waves crashed over him, and he crawled out of the water.

While the men loaded the box holding Silas into a wagon, I stumbled over to Hinsworth. He was staring up at the night sky, one arm flung over his face, panting.

"You can't just leave them there!" I cried, the taste of rage bitter on my tongue.

Hinsworth gazed up at me, blinking. "There are more lifeboats coming. The animals are on them."

"They're not animals!"

Hinsworth shot out his hand, grabbed my ankle, and squeezed. "They are what I say they are," he growled. A cold, wet finger, gritty with sand, stroked my skin.

I yanked my foot away and nearly fell over.

"You'll pay in hell for what you've done," I hissed.

Hinsworth chuckled, a low humorless sound. He pushed himself to his feet, his body swaying slightly. A horse-drawn wagon rumbled up. I watched him walk away on unsteady feet and pull himself up next to the driver. They disappeared into the fog.

With nothing else to do but wait, I thought of Javier. Being with him had been beautiful, peaceful, complicated. But one feeling ruled them all. Guilt. If anyone outside the family were to find out about us, it would be Javier who would suffer the most.

My father had warned me a life with Javier was not possible—me a Carillo and he a "lowly farmworker." But to my heart and eyes, Javier had never been just that. His good looks were undeniable, but it was his kindness and quiet intelligence that drew me to him. He was the only one willing to accept me and the mark on my back.

When I fled in tears from my brother and his endless torments, it had been Javier who found me, pulled me aside, and whispered, "He's a nobody, mi amor. His words are nothing."

My mind wandered back to our last night together. I could still feel his hands on my skin, his tender kisses. But even amid our passion, worry gnawed at me. My parents were dead. My uncle lived far away. And I'd known if Nestor caught me with Javier, he wouldn't stand for it.

And he hadn't. It was all my fault.

The distant clip-clop of approaching horses jolted me back to the foreign, lonely shore. The damp sand leeched the heat from my body. The pain of losing Javier pierced my heart like a sharp blade. I cried, imagining the water swallowing him, still trapped in that cage, dragging him and the others into the depths.

A lone horseback rider appeared and told me help was on the way, men and wagons to carry whatever could be salvaged from the ship.

My wits were dulled by our terrifying escape and my fear that Javier and the others had drowned, so I only nodded in acknowledgment that he'd spoken.

"Where were you going?" he asked, looking out at the water, gripping the reins of his horse.

"San Francisco." My voice was hoarse. "Is this San Francisco?"

"Not even close," he replied. "You're just north of Monterey."

"Then what is this place?"

In the darkness, I couldn't get a good look at the man's face, but the set of his shoulders and the gruffness of his voice suggested he was spry but no longer young.

He laughed grimly. "Devil's Landing. It's a treacherous bit of coastline, and no spot more so than right here. The rocks and the fog are enough to give the best captain grief. They're saying everyone made it off the ship, though." He paused and cleared his throat. "You shouldn't be out here by your lonesome. Why don't you come back with me? I live close by. The missus can fix you up with dry clothes and such."

"Thank you," I said. "But I need to wait."

He cleared his throat again. "I heard the ship was carrying circus people. Are you with the circus too?"

I choked down a sob. "Yes."

"I've never seen a circus," the man replied. "Now *that* would be something. I've heard about those contortionists, I think they're called. Do you have some of those?"

My English failed me. I didn't know what that was, and I was in no mood to ask. "No," I said.

"How about one of those fellows that swallows swords?"

"I don't know. I just joined. At the last port."

I could feel his gaze grow more curious. "Is that right? Now what is it that you do? Walk a tightrope?"

Without money, I had no choice but to stay with the circus. As meager as the pay was, I'd need it, in a country where I knew no one. Even if I could get a letter home, asking for help, my brother would laugh and rip it to pieces.

Could the circus continue after the shipwreck? I supposed it depended on how much could be salvaged before the boat was lost to the sea. The troupe had survived, but it was hard to imagine a circus without a tent and all the equipment that went with it.

I shuddered, thinking about the costume that made me look nude and the prospect of showing the scar on my back to paying strangers.

"I guess you don't do that either," the man said when I didn't reply, sounding disappointed. "How about wild animals?" he asked a moment later. "Now *that* would really be something."

A lump squeezed my throat, and I had to swallow hard to keep from crying.

A sound from the fog caught my attention, so I rose and walked toward the water. My teeth chattered, and I watched the three boats approach the shore. The cries of the seagulls overhead, the smell of salt in the air.

When I saw the shackled creatures among the miserable crew, I stumbled into the frigid surf and shouted "Javier!" but Strongman Jack jumped out and pulled me away.

"These animals are dangerous, Miss Carillo," he said, not unkindly. "You don't want to get too close."

I pounded his broad chest with my fists. "They're not animals," I wept. "They're men. I know them. They were taken from my farm in Mexico by señor Hinsworth. He did something to them."

Jack's thick black eyebrows furrowed. He looked beyond me to the wagons waiting to ferry cargo and people to the harbor.

He placed a firm hand on my shoulder. "It's been a long night. You shouldn't be out here. Let's get you somewhere warm."

Too distraught to argue, I stepped around him and ran toward the boats bobbing in the choppy water. I could see the men Jack called animals, but I couldn't recognize Javier. Not anymore. He was a creature, a chain around his neck. The realization unleashed a wail from my soul. Tears welled in my eyes, blurring my vision as I charged through the surf.

The creature closest to me reared up and, pulling against its chains, hissed.

I stumbled back, falling into the water. A wave crashed over me. I managed to stand up, sputtering, the saltwater tasting like tears.

Hands grabbed me under my arms and dragged me back onto the sand. Jack stood between me and the boats, legs planted wide, hands on his hips.

"Let's not add a drowning to the night we've had," he said sternly.

The reality of it all crashed down on me. Javier was a man no longer. Jack was right. He'd become an animal.

The anguish was overwhelming. My screams echoed through the early morning darkness, and tears streamed down my face. Tears for what the Hinsworth brothers had done to Javier, tears for my new life on foreign soil without him.

To my surprise, Hinsworth announced he was paying for the women to stay at a hotel at Devil's Landing for a few days, to wash up and recover until the tents could be dried out and set up. The men would camp out in the storage building at the other end of the dock. All except for Jacopo. He stayed at the hotel too, in the best room they had to offer. That was another surprise. The Lion Lord came from a wealthy family and had plenty of money to spend as he wished. As long as he stayed away, Ewa explained, his father was happy to fund his adventures. His father was a successful businessman, and

Jacopo's hairy condition had been an embarrassment, especially after a newspaper called him the "millionaire's werewolf son."

"But why did he join the circus?" I asked.

Ewa gave me an odd look. "Where else would he be so welcome?"

It felt good to bathe in hot water and wash the salt from my skin and hair. Many of us arrived wet and bloody, and when the proprietor saw us, he cried out and said he'd fetch a doctor, believing us injured from the wreck. The blood from our menstruation had no consideration for shipwrecks, and our skirts were a mess. We were too exhausted to be embarrassed.

Hinsworth surprised me again by paying for a wagon to drive us to Monterey, where we were to buy enough clothes to replace those ruined or lost.

Monterey was an interesting, lively town, and I would have loved to spend more time there exploring it. As we ate lunch in a restaurant and drank tea, I realized I had barely given Javier a thought. My stomach churned. How selfish I was, having a meal, a free woman, while he was still caged and suffering.

"I should have done something," I whispered to Ewa when we walked back to the hotel.

A bandage around her forehead covered the gash she'd received during her fall on the ship. She was still pale but, with the assistance of the new cane she'd purchased in Monterey, was able to walk on her own.

"What's done is done, my dear," she said.

Words I would remember later with great bitterness.

Chapter 17

In the cold, damp fog of Devil's Landing, Hinsworth gathered us together to make an announcement. His yellow hair was disheveled and thick from salt water. There were dark circles under his eyes, but his shoulders and mouth had a determined set to them.

"We'll be staying here for a bit before we move on," he said. "San Francisco is a big city, with a population accustomed to the best in entertainment, so we will use this time to make sure we're ready. After all, we have new acts to work on." He glowered in my direction.

Everyone stared at me.

"What's she going to do anyway?" Jack said to the man standing next to him.

"A Mexican dance, I heard," the acrobat replied.

Louella bristled. "We do the *real* dancing. She's an amateur."

Hinsworth brought his hands together in a thunderous clap. "There are no amateurs in my circus." He paused, his eyebrows coming together, and he glanced my way again. His look held a warning that said, *Do not disappoint me.*

Hinsworth scratched the side of his face before continuing.

"Captain Pendergrast and his men have moved to Monterey, except for one." He made a sweeping gesture with his hand.

My eyes followed the motion and landed on a figure standing off to the side. My heart lifted at the sight of him.

"That's Liam," Hinsworth said. "He'll be joining us. If he can climb a mast and do all those things he did in the air on a moving ship, he can walk a tightrope. Or so he assures me."

Liam dipped his head. Louella preened and inched closer to him.

I was glad he was staying on.

Hinsworth cleared his throat. "There's another thing. Our circus is smaller than some of the others, but no less great. Our show is unusual. It appeals to discriminating tastes. But there's one thing we've never had, and I've always regretted it. We've never had an animal act. Well, we have one now."

The crowd exchanged knowing looks, and heads bent together in whispered reaction.

Ewa grasped my wrist and squeezed it hard. "Say nothing if you want to stay on," she hissed into my ear.

I bit my lip and glared at Hinsworth instead.

If he noticed, he didn't show it. "We got ourselves the rarest of beasts in Mexico. It took a special expedition and a good amount of money to track them down in the forest." He paused long enough to glance over at a low building in the distance, lip curling. "I'm training them myself. It's difficult work, and while we're at it, I don't want anyone near them or their cages."

Louella waved a hand over her head. "What kind of animals are they, Mr. Hinsworth?"

Hinsworth shoved his hands into the pockets of his vest. "Can't answer that, I'm afraid. The beasts are a rare species, never been seen in public before." He tapped his chin thoughtfully. "Two arms, two legs, more like an ape than a tiger, but much fiercer."

Louella cleared her throat. "So, you'll keep them chained and in cages, then?" she asked in an unnaturally high voice.

"You've just given me an idea. No cages. That would be something to say." He laughed. "No cages can hold our beasts!"

He reached behind his back, produced a whip, and cracked it overhead.

"Be prepared for rehearsals beginning Friday. But also, be prepared for an audience. We're doing three shows for the good people of Devil's Landing. Full costume, complete performances, including the new ones: Liam the Death-Defying Wire Walker, señorita Bonita's mesmerizing Dance of the Demon, and of course, The Strange and Savage Beasts."

He cracked his whip again as the crowd applauded.

"A few of the men and I will be with the beasts for the rest of the day, and we expect to be left alone. If you need anything, see Ewa." And with those final words, he nodded at Jack to follow him and strode off.

My legs trembled beneath me as I imagined Hinsworth's whip striking Javier and the others. On the ship, the poor men had been treated like animals, but with the performances starting Friday, their suffering would only become more unbearable.

"HB has no experience training animals," Frieda said.

Jacopo gave a little shrug. "It doesn't take a genius to do that. Just a whip and a strong personality. He'll get it done. Let's just hope he doesn't kill them in the process."

Chapter 18

Devil's Landing was a small fishing village with cabins, a hotel, a saloon, a market, a laundry owned by a Chinese family, and a post office. For an isolated place, it was surprisingly busy, and at first, I couldn't account for it. Then Liam explained it was a whaling and fishing port.

Dairy farms dotted the land on either side of the marsh flowing into the harbor. Sheep and cows, mostly. The farmer's wives sold fresh milk and cheese but sent the bulk of their wares to Monterey, so if you didn't make your purchases by noon, you'd have to wait until the following day.

The hotel was not fancy. The wood siding was faded and peeling from the damp air, but the rooms were clean, and it was good to sleep in a proper bed.

The red and white circus tents went up in a field, lending a jaunty air to the harbor filled with tall masts and rough men. The women of the troupe moved to sleeping tents, and while the cots were sturdy enough, I missed the comfort of the hotel. Hinsworth paid the proprietor for our continued use of its lavatory and bathroom, which had a proper clawfoot tub and hot water.

The men were forced to rough it, washing in a low, drafty building with the visiting whalers. There was plenty of grumbling about the cold water.

Liam fit in well with the circus people, which Ewa said was unusual. I'd found most of the troupe to be clannish, with little time for newcomers, but Jack and the other men invited Liam to drink with them at the saloon and to play cards, or whatever it was they did after dark. Drinking and telling stories, according to Liam, who whispered he'd discovered Hinsworth had rented a cabin for his brother at the far end of the harbor. Liam never mentioned my scar again, and gradually, I found myself relaxing in his presence. He was unfailingly kind and friendly.

I told him nothing of what I'd witnessed below deck—Silas going into the locked room holding Javier and the others. Not because I didn't trust him, but because it was such an outlandish story, he was sure to think me unwell. I was also ashamed to admit I'd known the truth about those cages all along.

Jack told Liam the training of "the beasts" was going better than Hinsworth had expected. Instead of resisting, they were strangely compliant. Jack even invited Liam to watch them practice, with Hinsworth in the role of Beast Trainer, but Liam came away unsettled.

"The way those things look at a person isn't right," he said. "But they're meek enough, what with HB and that whip of his. He's free with the lash, and they've got the marks to prove it, the poor devils."

"It's barbaric," I replied, my insides twisting.

"That it is," Liam agreed. "I hope the act is ready by Friday. Those things are all the fishermen talk about. Seeing those beasts in the show."

Ewa painted an advertisement for the circus and had lithographs printed in Monterey. Signs went up everywhere—poles, fences, shop windows, and the post office. Outside the harbor, they appeared on barns, in nearby towns, and as far away as Monterey. The lithographs were brightly colored and showed a strange, hairy creature standing on an enormous balancing ball, glaring in a menacing manner.

Boys, bursting with excitement, tried to get a glimpse of the performers. But it was the beasts they really hoped to see.

Ewa tasked me with arranging for food to sell at the circus. My English was good enough to get the job done, though I sometimes had to repeat myself to be understood. Still, the local women were kind enough and asked what life had been like in Mexico and how I had come to join the circus.

"To see the world," I lied.

Three days. Three days until I was to perform for the first time in front of an audience, dancing for money.

I had been practicing my routine with Ewa, but Hinsworth insisted on seeing me perform before Friday, and my nerves were getting the better of me. The prospect of dancing in front of him made my chest feel as if something were sitting on it.

"Why can't he just see it on Friday?" I asked during a break.

The musicians had gone outside to smoke.

Ewa was stretched out on a divan the strongmen had brought from the hotel. She gave me a stern look. "This circus belongs to HB, and he has every right to see your performance before you make your debut."

Jacopo, playing solitaire at a table, looked up. "What Ewa is really saying is that she took a chance on you, and you better not disappoint HB because nobody likes to be around him when he's less than pleased." He shivered, as if remembering past experiences.

Ewa put a hand to her forehead and sighed. "Do you think she'll be able to pull this off, Jackie?"

Jacopo paused before replying. "What Miss Carillo lacks in the fine art of dancing will hardly be noticed, not with the dress she'll be wearing and that…atrocity on her back." He grimaced. "HB will love it."

My heart sank.

Ewa pushed a stray lock of auburn hair from her face. "Oh dear. The man has such strange appetites. I'd forgotten about that."

The Lion Lord snorted disdainfully. "Fetishes, Ewa. They are called fetishes."

Chapter 19

If I hadn't needed the wages from the circus, I would have fled the moment Hinsworth entered the tent. He remained standing, legs planted wide, thumbs in his belt.

"All right," he said. "Let's see it, then."

He was doing his best to look bored, but I wasn't fooled. And neither was Jacopo, who gave my arm a little squeeze of encouragement.

"Pretend he's not here," he whispered in my ear.

That was impossible to do. Even from across the tent, I could smell the whiskey on his breath and feel the heat of his stare.

Ewa clapped her hands, and the musicians began to play. I stepped forward, trying not to think of my flesh-colored dress, focusing instead on the dance.

As I moved to the rhythm of the music, Hinsworth's unyielding gaze bore into me. I swallowed hard and pushed through the routine, refusing to betray my discomfort. My dance combined the flamboyant steps of my homeland with the moves Jacopo had taught me—every twist and turn precise, every movement sultry but deliberate. The fabric of my dress caressed my skin and swirled around my bare legs.

When I glanced over at Hinsworth, his eyes trailed up and down my body, and I felt a hot flush creeping up my neck. But

I didn't falter. If Hinsworth didn't approve of the act, I would lose my job and would be alone and poor in a foreign land.

When the dance neared the end, I slid off the cape hiding the horror on my back, but I couldn't bring myself to turn and show him.

Ewa cracked her cane against the table. "Show him, Ana Maria."

The musicians faltered for a moment, then resumed with a new, nervous energy. I swallowed, raised my hands over my head, fingers fluttering, and turned.

Behind me, Hinsworth gasped. "What the devil is that?" he said, his voice like gravel.

The music stopped.

All eyes were on me now. It was the first time the musicians had seen the entire act. They shuffled their feet nervously, shock in their eyes.

"Just a scar, Ambrose," Jacopo said lightly.

Hinsworth stood, transfixed, eyes wide with disbelief, but I saw something else too. Fear.

"What…What is it?" he asked again, this time directing his question at me. "How did you get it?"

Ewa stepped forward and placed a hand on his arm. "It's not what you think, Ambrose. It's not a mark. It was an accident. A burn."

He shook his head, eyes narrowing. "That's a mark if ever I saw one."

Hinsworth said nothing more. He spun around and strode out of the tent, Ewa hobbling after him.

I should have been pleased to see Hinsworth so unnerved. Instead, I paced, worrying it meant my time with the circus was about to end. Ewa was gone for a long time. When she returned more than an hour later, she slumped into a chair.

"Ambrose approved," she finally said. "Said you're much better than our pantomime act." She paused. "But he wants you to move a little more…suggestively. He thought it was a bit too tame."

"What about the women? The children?"

She shrugged. "A little more with the hips ought to do it, and if you can, try a coquettish look or two. No reason to look like you're dancing at a funeral."

We ran through my act a few more times, and when Ewa was finally satisfied, I said, "I wouldn't have thought señor Hinsworth would be such a superstitious man."

Ewa eyed me warily. "He was just surprised, that's all."

"But he believes in magic."

Ewa's violet irises went wide, a hand coming to her chest. "Oh, be careful, my dear. That's not something you want to let HB catch you saying. He doesn't tolerate those kinds of rumors."

"The rumors about his brother?" I persisted.

Ewa's face made it clear she'd had enough of my questions. She snatched up her cane and wagged it in my direction. "Especially his brother."

Chapter 20

The night of the first performance at Devil's Landing was fast approaching, and there was an air of excitement. We practiced our acts together for the first time. All except for The Savage and Strange Beasts.

Most of the troupe didn't seem happy with Hinsworth's decision not to rehearse with us before the live show.

"We've never had any animals," one of the musicians grumbled. "What if loud noises scare them?"

"What if they don't like painted faces?" said the clown named Augustus. "There are all kinds of things that could go wrong with an animal act."

"HB still isn't thinking about doing the act without a cage, is he?" Louella laced up her white boots. "What if they try to attack us? Who will stop them?"

The questions haunted me into the night. I'd failed to free Javier, and now it was too late. I was just another member of Hinsworth's circus, dependent on him for my survival.

On Thursday night, I fell into a restless sleep, exhausted after a long day of rehearsing under the big tent. Louella had made a show of turning her back whenever I revealed my scar during my act.

Her reaction worried me. If a woman who'd seen all manner of curiosities seemed so upset by my terrible scar, wouldn't it be too much for the audience? Jacopo said they had thought of that and had a plan but wouldn't tell me what it was.

Friday morning arrived, for once, without the thick mist usually plaguing the harbor. There were little boys everywhere, and some girls too. The opening of the circus was a big event, and it seemed they'd come to Devil's Landing instead of going to school.

I picked at my supper. Frieda joked it was a good thing I had so little appetite. Ruth had taken in my dress—at Hinsworth's instruction—and it wouldn't allow me to eat a regular meal without busting the seams.

When I saw Liam walking toward me, his face nearly as red as his costume, I couldn't help but laugh. Hinsworth had ordered a change for him too. His well-muscled legs, arms, and chest were bare. He was wearing short bloomers and a shirt that opened in a deep V, a thick gold belt around his waist.

"HB said I had to wear this," Liam announced, looking miserable. He tugged on the bottom of his bloomers, but that only revealed more of his torso. It took some getting used to, seeing everyone so scantily clad. Everyone except for Ewa, Jacopo, and the musicians.

"Is there a net?" I asked, imagining him crashing to the ground.

He shook his head. "For the girls doing the trapeze, there's a net. But not for me."

"That's…lunacy," I cried.

Liam grinned. "That's me. A lunatic. I climbed masts, and those were much higher, and there was no net to catch me if I fell. And there will be no wind or rain in my face, and no ship rocking back and forth either." When he noticed the extent of my alarm, he added, "I'll be fine, Miss."

After we ate, I walked around the village. The sky and sea blended in a blue haze. Waves lapped against the dock. Seagulls flew above, calling out as they circled the fishing boats, diving into the water for scraps.

At the end of the harbor, I stood looking out at the sea, thinking of home and wondering if I'd ever see it again.

Over the rumble of the surf and the lonely cries of the gulls came a distant shouting from the drab building where Hinsworth kept Javier and the others. It was set far back from the road on a grassy berm. Despite Hinsworth's warnings to stay away, I felt my feet dragging me closer and closer, my heart thundering in my chest. The sounds sharpened—the lashing of a whip followed by pitiful wails.

The hovel was crudely constructed. I inched toward the building, my skin crawling with dread. Peering between the wooden slats, I saw an abominable scene unfolding.

Hinsworth standing tall, a whip clutched in his fist, looming over a body huddled in a corner. Five other creatures, cloaked in dark fur, cowered together. Three men brandished long poles, forcing them into a tight circle, like helpless prey.

My vision blurred. I registered the new, monstrous changes that had befallen them. Their legs were shorter, arms longer, torsos strangely elongated, and their features blended into their flattened faces.

Javier was unrecognizable. A violent chill swept over me as I beheld the man I once loved, the man who was no more.

I choked down the cry rising in me, like a tidal wave of grief and terror. But only a broken sob escaped my throat.

Hinsworth snapped his head up and swiveled it in my direction.

"No one had better be out there," he thundered.

By the time one of the men came to investigate, I was racing away down the hill.

Chapter 21

The circus had begun. I watched from behind a curtain, thinking about the dark magic that had transformed Javier into a beast and the man forcing him to perform like an exotic animal. I no longer hoped to restore those poor souls back to their former selves.

With the show underway, there was little time to indulge my grief. The curtain opened, and I was pulled into a world of vibrant colors and jaunty tunes.

The big tent smelled of fresh roasted peanuts, popcorn, and fried fish sandwiches.

Hinsworth greeted the crowd, promising an unforgettable evening, then he disappeared through a flap and was replaced by Jacopo.

The pantomime girls performed a few musical numbers, kicking up their shapely legs. Strongman Jack entered and threw them over his shoulders, as if they weighed nothing, carrying them away while the crowd roared with laughter. Augustus the clown invited two fishermen onto the stage. They nervously agreed, perching on chairs. Jack grabbed both chairs and lifted them high in the air, astounding everyone with his strength.

A drum roll announced the next act: the Kastbar Sisters. The spotlight drew the audience's attention upward, and there were Frieda and her sisters, wearing silk tights and short diaphanous skirts, smiling down at the crowd. To a burst of applause, they scrambled even higher up the poles until they reached the top, grabbed horizontal bars dangling from ropes, and hurled themselves into the air. How they didn't collide, I didn't know. I watched, holding my breath, as they twisted and spun around, doing summersaults in the air, their long blond hair gradually loosening and swinging free.

Liam followed, and I had to look away. He walked a cord stretched over the stage, one foot dipping on either side as he made his way across.

"He's doing it without a balance bar," Jacopo hissed.

"Oh." I had a hand pressed against my mouth.

"He's been practicing seven hours a day," Jacopo said.

Liam began doing tricks, and I gasped. He sprang to his feet, followed by a backward summersault.

Beside me, Jacopo clapped a hand to his forehead. "Oh no, he's not ready to do it forward."

I didn't understand and said so.

"Backward is easier." He clutched my arm. "He can see where the wire is before he lands. Forward is much more dangerous."

We watched, our heads bent together, hardly daring to breathe, but Liam was once again standing, arms outstretched, his expression victorious.

The music shifted, becoming a tango. Augustus the clown climbed up a ladder and handed Liam a red cape. Liam tied it around his neck and began dancing upon the wire.

When he was done, the audience stood, stomped their feet, and clapped.

Louella had come to stand nearby. She too was transfixed. "He has the perfect build," she said. "He's just wonderful!"

Jacopo introduced Ofelia, the Goddess of the Iron Jaw, magnificent in a short white costume trimmed in gold. I had not seen her act during rehearsals. Her performance and strength were astounding to behold. She dangled in the air, teeth gripping an iron and leather bit. When she swung, Augustus the clown hurtled himself at the woman and clung to her legs. The audience screamed, expecting him to be dropped. But Ofelia held him firmly, then exchanged her burden for Strongman Jack.

Two more acts went by in a blur. Finally, it was my turn. Jacopo announced my act.

"And now, ladies, gentlemen, and children, all the way from Mexico, señorita Bonita, performing her never-before-seen Dance of the Demon."

Jacopo led me to the center of the stage and hooked his arm through mine.

"But before she begins, I must warn you, her dance includes something that is not for the faint of heart. Some fear what you are about to see may cause hysteria or even demonic possession. It is in accordance with the laws of this great nation, and with the advice of medical doctors, that I am compelled to offer you something to protect you from its effects. You have no obligation to purchase this protection, but we will accept no responsibility for the wellbeing of those who choose not to."

Whispers rippled through the crowd.

Ewa appeared and waved a bit of red string in the air. "These are special bracelets created for the purpose of protecting you from any evil outcomes from what you are about to behold. They are yours for the same cost as a bag of peanuts."

Boys ran down the aisles with coins, returning clutching the red strings.

The audience eyed me nervously. When Ewa first told me about the scheme, it bothered me, but I no longer cared, too focused on getting through the next few minutes.

The music began. At first, my arms and legs didn't want to cooperate. I felt stiff, exposed in my tight dress in front of all those strangers. Wishing I could close my eyes and shut them all out, I looked inward instead, thinking of the time I'd sneaked a dance with Javier in the stable back home while two boys played guitar. I longed for the comfort of his hand pressed against my back, but I was alone on that stage, about to reveal my shameful secret.

The music swelled around me, and I moved my body, skirt swirling, hips and arms in sync with the beat. People leaned forward in their seats, captivated.

As the music picked up, I began to move faster, twirling and spinning. The crowd erupted into applause, and I felt a surge of energy, lost in the moment.

And then the music stopped.

It was time.

Taking a deep breath, I reached back and unhooked the clasp of my small cape, letting it drop to the floor.

As Jacopo had shown me, I raised my hands with a flourish of my wrists and slowly turned in a circle. The audience gasped.

"It's the evil eye!" a woman cried.

The evil eye. The evil eye. The evil eye. The words echoed around me.

Jacopo stepped forward and urged everyone to hold their wrists in the air. "The bracelets are more powerful if you hold them up. That's it. It's not too late to buy one. Do not worry, ma'am. A boy is walking over to you now. We have enough for everyone."

Silence fell over the crowd, and they stared in disbelief at my back. I lifted my chin and looked out, seeing fear in some eyes but also pity and even respect in others.

Then the music began again, and it was over. People jumped to their feet, clapping, emboldened by their red bracelets and relieved they had survived the evil eye marking my skin.

"Take a bow." Jacopo scooped up my cape and draped it over my shoulders.

I did, and then I was behind the curtain with Ewa, Frieda and her sisters, Jack, and Augustus. They all surrounded me with smiles, then hugs. Even Louella gave me a grudging nod of acceptance.

Only Liam looked stricken. "It's real, then?" he asked in a quiet voice.

He hadn't seen any of my rehearsals.

I bit my lip and swallowed. "It's real. But it's just a scar."

Liam nodded solemnly. Then he brightened. "Louella will get herself one, you watch, now that your act is more popular than hers."

Chapter 22

Jacopo dashed past me and leapt onto the stage. "And now, the act you've all been waiting for. It's not the largest menagerie. We have no lions or tigers, no bears nor elephants. Camels and hippos you will not see here tonight. We have no traveling zoo. What we have…" He let his voice drift off for dramatic effect, holding a hand over his eyes as if searching for something. "What we have is what we promised you. The most daring collection of living wild beasts in captivity. Rare creatures found only in the jungles of Mexico."

Drums rolled, this time louder and more dramatic than before. The Lion Lord walked in a circle, arms stretched into the air.

"And now, it is my great honor to introduce the man who dared to capture and train them. The beast hunter and beast tamer, Ambrose Hinsworth."

Smoke filled the stage, and out of the haze stepped Hinsworth. The audience gasped. And I did too.

For there he stood, legs planted wide, a tall black hat on his head, his face made nearly unrecognizable by a layer of chalky white paint.

"Bless me," Frieda whispered beside me.

The paint had settled into the lines around his nose and mouth, making him appear older than his years. Rouge stained his cheeks and lips, smudged beyond their natural lines. Gray paste on his eyelids added to his fiendish appearance.

In contrast with the whiteness of his face, his hair appeared as yellow as the sun. He strutted onto the stage, his tight jacket emphasizing the breadth of his shoulders. Walking in a circle, he glowered, as if displeased by secret thoughts. As if the audience weren't there.

And then his head snapped up. He seemed to notice he wasn't alone, and a slow grin came to his face.

Lifting his chin, he bellowed, "Come to see the beasts, I hear!"

The audience responded with thunderous applause and cries of anticipation. People began to chant.

"Beasts! Beasts! Bring out the beasts!"

Hinsworth lifted his hat and gave an exaggerated bow, scraping his top hat along the ground. When he straightened, the smile was gone. A sneer replaced it.

"Oh, they'll come. They will. But are you ready? I don't think you're ready for what you're about to see."

"We're ready," the audience screamed. "We're ready!" Feet pounded and hands waved in the air.

I shivered, watching Hinsworth taunt the audience.

He paced with the restless swagger of a lion, whipping the audience into a frenzy. I caught his eye. He paused, and in a long, slow swipe of his long tongue, he licked his lips, then winked.

"Oh, he's in a mood." Jacopo stood so close to my ear, I felt the soft hair on his face tickle my skin.

Strongman Jack and two others rolled a large cage onto the stage, its contents hidden by black fabric. The audience grew silent.

Hinsworth strutted to the cage and, with a flick of his wrist, yanked away the tarp.

Gasps filled the tent. A woman shrieked.

Gone were the meek creatures I'd seen the day before. They seemed to have gone through another transformation, for they now appeared wild and dangerous, with snarling faces. Razor-sharp teeth and yellow eyes glowed in the dimness of the tent.

Hinsworth strode off the stage and disappeared behind a curtain. The musicians exchanged uncertain looks. Whatever was happening was not part of the act they'd rehearsed. Hinsworth reappeared a few moments later, wearing a voluminous cape, his straight back now strangely humped.

When I glanced over at Ewa, her face was so white I thought she might faint. Jacopo pressed a hand to his stomach as if it hurt.

The hump on Hinsworth's back seemed to be moving. The crowd began to whisper and point, but Hinsworth ignored them.

The drummer began a slow, ominous rhythm. Hinsworth stood in front of the cage, his white-painted face twisted into a cold smile. He raised a whip, and it hit the ground with a loud crack. There were stools inside the cage. A beast crouched on each one. They opened their mouths, and out came horrible, high-pitched screeches.

A wave of nausea hit me. My beloved had become a monster. A horrifying, unrecognizable brute. I whispered his name under my breath and cursed the dark magic that had changed him.

The sound of drums grew louder and louder, a steady pounding in my ears. A bead of sweat trickled down my back. The creatures bent and twisted upon their stools, contorting in impossible ways, as if they had no bones, snapping their jaws at Hinsworth.

He reached toward the cage door. A woman in the audience screamed, "No!" and Hinsworth whirled around.

"No! Who said 'no?'" His eyes scanned the crowd.

Whispers rippled through the audience, but no one spoke up.

"Who…said…no?" he demanded.

"It's all part of the act," a man shouted.

Moments later, another voice chimed in. "You heard him. It's all part of the act."

Hinsworth looked disgusted. He walked across the stage, arms folded across his chest, sulking like a child. He reminded me of my brother, Nestor.

Then he held his hands out in supplication. "What's it going to be? Shall I release the beasts or not? Are you too afraid? Or is your curiosity stronger than your fear? Will your lust for excitement overcome your intellect?"

Children began to whimper. A mother rushed a crying girl out of the tent.

The hump on his back was moving. Hinsworth slapped it, and it went still.

"What's on his back?" I asked, turning to Ewa.

She gave me a long look. "What do you think?"

I knew. Of course, I knew. The word came loose from my mouth. "Silas."

She gave a tight nod, then went back to staring at the stage. The floor seemed to tilt under me. Hinsworth never brought his brother into the public. He kept him hidden away, first below deck, then off in a cabin somewhere in Devil's Landing. But tonight, Hinsworth had strapped him to his back and hidden him under his cloak.

Did Hinsworth need Silas? Need his magic to keep the beasts under control? Or to keep them…beasts? To make them as fierce as they now appeared yet harmless to their tamer?

I stared at the animals, studying their features, trying to figure out which one had been Javier, but I couldn't. There was nothing in those creatures I recognized. Javier's smooth brown skin, the strong hands with long, nimble fingers, the slight hook of his nose that made him so beautiful in profile—it was all gone. Stolen, like his life.

Hinsworth opened the door and entered the cage.

The beasts recoiled on their stools. Hinsworth raised the whip. The beasts jerked their heads back as if they were puppets on a string. Goosebumps rose all over my skin.

With a crack of the whip, Hinsworth gave the creatures a little bow, then retreated to the door of the cage.

I saw what the audience could not. A small, pale face ringed with golden curls appeared briefly from under the cloak. Tiny white fingers wriggled in the air.

The beasts saw Silas too, and they hissed, then quieted. Silas disappeared under the folds of the fabric.

He'd used neither whip nor club, but whatever he had done seemed to break their spirits. They slid off the stools and dropped to their knees, heads bent.

Hinsworth stepped out of the cage, leaving the door open. He clapped his hands and yelled, "Up, up, rise up!"

One by one, the creatures slinked through the open door. The crowd pressed back against their seats with a collective gasp.

The beasts rose, slowly and awkwardly, as if unsure how to work their limbs. Hinsworth turned in a circle, pointing upward, and suddenly, the beasts were running.

For one horrible moment, I feared they were headed toward the audience, but instead, they raced for the tent poles, shimmying up, one hand over another, pushing up with their feet with astonishing agility. When they reached the top, their heads brushing the canvas, they hung there, staring down at the people below them.

Silas's head peeked out again for just a moment. Everyone was too busy gaping at the spectacle of the beasts to notice, but I saw him. His eyes were glazed over, and his mouth was moving. So were his fingers again.

The beasts threw their heads back. Their ear-piercing screeches filled the tent, and the people in the audience clapped their hands over their ears. It was the sound of nightmares. Tears slid down my face. Hinsworth cracked the whip again, and the beasts slid down, their feet hitting the ground so hard their knees buckled.

Children buried their faces in their mothers' laps. Wives clutched their husbands' arms. Several men looked ready to leap to their feet to defend their loved ones, should the beasts bolt from the stage and attack.

Hinsworth's reverie broke. He looked out at the audience, as if suddenly aware of the people, and he held up a hand of reassurance. "It's all right everyone. It's all right." Then he cracked his whip and pointed at the cage door.

To my surprise—and the crowd's great relief—the beasts shuffled back inside. Hinsworth pulled the cage door shut, then made a big show of locking it.

The audience erupted in applause. More from relief than joy, I thought.

Hinsworth had just taken his third and final bow, top hat in one hand, blond hair nearly touching the floor, when he lurched to the side and toppled over, a shrill cry coming from the hump on his back.

Chapter 23

Strongman Jack carried Hinsworth off the stage, pushing through the curtains and setting him down on a rubber mat. I was standing closest and had a quick glimpse of the small head. Jack quickly pulled Hinsworth's cloak and covered it.

He stood and leaned toward me. "You didn't see that," Jack said in a low voice.

Everyone gathered around, eyes wide. Ewa lowered herself to the ground to attend to Hinsworth.

Sweat had made a messy smear of the chalky white paint on Hinsworth's face, revealing patches of bloodless skin below. Even in unconscious repose, his lips seemed to sneer. Ewa glanced up with a scowl and waved at Jacopo.

"Don't just stand there," she snapped. "Go out and tell the audience everything is all right. And remind them to tell their friends and neighbors about tomorrow night's performance!"

"But is he all right?" Louella asked, pressing her hands together. "We can't have another show without him."

Hinsworth stirred.

"Of course, he's all right." But Ewa's voice betrayed her uncertainty.

The hump began to wriggle.

Ewa clapped her hands. "Now go! Do as I say."

A few minutes later, the crowd gone and the tent empty, I felt a change in the air. The festive circus atmosphere turned into something ominous. A screech made us jump. It was followed by another. The beasts were on the other side of the curtain, momentarily forgotten.

Ewa turned to Jack. "Are they secure? We can't have them getting out."

"I'll find a few men, and we'll get them to the building," he replied, then sprinted away. Jack moved surprisingly fast for a man of his size.

I was turning to leave when Ewa grabbed my skirt. Lowering her voice, she said, "Not you. I need your help. Go to the tent. Under my bed, there is a bag. Bring it to me."

I found her traveling bag and rushed back to the tent. A tinkling sound came from inside. Bottles, I realized. And then I remembered. While we were in Monterey, Ewa had visited Chinese shops, buying herbs and cures to replace those she'd lost aboard the *Iron Maiden.*

A lock of auburn hair fell over her face. Ewa plucked out a small bottle, removed the top, and plunged a dropper into the liquid.

"What's that?"

Ewa was so focused on her task, she didn't hear me. She released a few drops of the liquid onto Hinsworth's lips. He gave a little moan and choked. Eyelids fluttering, he tried to sit up, but the weight of his brother on his back held him down.

"Help me," Ewa said. "We need to get this off him."

This. Not *him.* It wasn't lost on me that Ewa couldn't bring herself to say, "Silas."

I dropped to my knees and untied the cape from Hinsworth's neck. The white paint stopped under his chin, and there was blood on his neck. Had one of the beasts gotten too close? No. The marks were too small to have been made by the beasts.

Ewa threw the cape aside, revealing the mystery below.

Silas was tightly bound onto his brother's back, snug in a leather sling attached to Hinsworth by a complicated arrangement of straps. His features were delicate, his skin porcelain, his mouth red and bow shaped. The hauntingly beautiful countenance of an angel, as cherubic as those adorning the church back home in San Sebastián.

Though their faces were similar, it was as if only Hinsworth had aged, his features thickening and maturing, while Silas remained frozen in youth. His neck was as slender as a little boy's. But his fingers made me shiver. Each ended in sharp, pointy nails, reddened with his brother's blood.

Muttering, Ewa dribbled a pale tincture onto a cloth and dabbed it against Hinsworth's wounds. I couldn't take my eyes off Silas, repulsed and fascinated. Although he made no sound, his mouth was moving, and his eyelids twitched.

"I told you not to do this," Ewa said to Hinsworth. She brushed away the yellow hair from his forehead.

"Didn't have a choice, did I?" Hinsworth replied, his eyes still closed.

Ewa's hand stilled on his forehead. "You chose this. You chose to bring Silas with you."

Hinsworth opened an eye. "I couldn't leave him behind. Not with what he can do."

Ewa sighed and looked away.

Liam wheeled Silas in a handcart to his cabin at the far end of the harbor. I helped Ewa walk Hinsworth to the hotel to await the doctor.

Ewa had discovered several deep gashes on his arms that needed sutures.

"How'd you get these?" Ewa demanded.

Hinsworth bit his lip and looked away. "I let my guard down during training, and the damn things had a go at me."

"It's lucky they didn't kill you," she muttered.

I wished they had.

The hotel owner invited us to wait for the doctor in the small saloon. Since most of the men preferred to drink at the bar, we were alone. Jacopo had complained of a terrible headache and retreated to his room. Ewa ordered us two glasses of sherry, but the owner returned with two glasses and the bottle.

After Ewa had finished her second glass, some color had returned to her face.

As casually as I could, I asked, "Were Silas and Hinsworth once…connected?"

Her mouth opened, then closed. She tipped her head up at the ceiling and gave a small, brittle laugh. "Aren't you a clever girl?"

I leaned forward, studying Ewa's beautiful face. In the glow of the lamps, the skin under her eyes looked slightly bruised. She drained the rest of her glass.

"You might as well know. It's not much of a secret anyway. Just remember, HB doesn't like people gossiping. Most of the troupe is new, so they haven't found out yet, but they will."

Ewa stared at the sherry bottle. I poured her another glass.

"Silas and Hinsworth were born attached twins," she said, "but HB got the better end of that bargain."

It was as I suspected.

"Silas was connected to Hinsworth's right hip. A doctor separated them a few years before I met HB in Liverpool. The surgery nearly killed them both. I didn't know them back then. But I'd heard about them, of course. Everybody had heard about the Hinsworths."

"Because they were attached?"

"Not just that. The Hinsworths are an old family, with lots of money and land. There were always rumors about the men. That they were able to summon demons to do their bidding and take revenge against anyone who stood in their way. They amassed property and collected beautiful women for their wives and mistresses."

A door opened, letting in the chilly night air. It wasn't the doctor but a guest, stumbling in from the saloon. He paused, and for a moment, I thought he'd try to join us. But after Ewa shot him a forbidding look, he tipped his hat and lurched away.

"Were all the Hinsworth men born with this ability?" I asked.

Ewa gave a tight nod. "By all accounts, yes." Her violet eyes glittered in the lamplight.

"So, Ambrose and Silas have the magic too?"

"They did. And they were quite powerful."

I stared at her for a long time. "Were?"

Ewa grimaced, as if she'd tasted something bitter. "When they were separated, Ambrose gained his freedom but lost his power. It all went to Silas." She paused and stared into her glass. "Silas didn't want the surgery, and he likes to punish Ambrose at every opportunity."

"He didn't want the surgery?"

"No. He was against it. And the doctor agreed. He said it was too risky, but Ambrose bribed him. Silas is still quite bitter about it. It makes him more dangerous than he already was." Ewa's cheeks were flushed, and she looked a bit tipsy.

"Is that why señor Hinsworth keeps Silas locked up?"

She nodded, not meeting my eyes. "Yes. Silas is very jealous. Especially of any women Ambrose becomes attached to. HB, for all his wanton ways, is a romantic. He fell in love with one of our acrobats years ago. She was young and beautiful. And one of the best I'd ever seen. HB was totally and completely besotted. But one day, she fell. Broke her neck and died."

"Did Silas…?"

Ewa shrugged. "He swears it was just an accident. But he was there the night it happened, watching the act."

It was hard to imagine Hinsworth in love. I felt the faintest stirrings of something like pity, until I remembered his heartless treatment of the man *I* loved. I pushed away my glass.

"Was Hinsworth making Silas do his magic tonight?" I asked slowly, struggling to understand. "To keep the…beasts under control?"

From Ewa's expression, I knew I had guessed right. "HB wouldn't have dared to let the beasts out of the cage without Silas's help. But Silas needs to see his subjects in order to control them. That's why HB hid him under his cloak."

I clutched Ewa's hand. "I heard them. On the ship. Silas didn't want to turn the men into…those things. But señor Hinsworth begged him." I pressed a hand against my head, trying to remember. "He said they needed it to happen. For the circus."

Ewa nodded again. "We're a small circus. There are bigger ones, with far more acts. We've struggled trying to attract crowds. HB believes we need something unusual, like rare and exotic beasts. He tried once. He bought an ape, and Silas did his magic, but it ended in disaster." Ewa squeezed her eyes shut and shuddered.

"What happened?"

Ewa tipped a little more sherry into her glass and swallowed it. "That monstrous creature killed HB's new fiancée. Ripped her head off. It's what caused most of the troupe to leave. It's only me, Jacopo, and Jack who are still around from those old days. And only because HB swore to keep Silas locked up."

My heart was beating so hard I pressed a hand against my chest. "And now, he's done it again. But not with animals. With people."

"God help us, he did."

In the silence that followed, a new thought occurred to me. Silas had the ability to turn ordinary men into horrible, violent beasts. So he must have the ability to do the reverse—turn the beasts back to the men they had once been.

A spark of hope jolted through my body. Perhaps I could convince Silas to undo the terrible wrongs he and his brother had committed against innocent humans.

A noise in the doorway made me jump.

It was the doctor, hat askew, holding a bag. Ewa used her cane to push herself to a standing position and led the man to Hinsworth's room.

Chapter 24

Hinsworth required many stitches, and the doctor gave him morphine for the pain. He left instructions that Hinsworth should not be left alone during the night. Which was how I came to be alone with that horrible man.

After the excitement of the evening, Ewa had taken ill. She'd not yet fully recovered from her fall on the *Iron Maiden* and was prone to headaches, making her weak and nauseous.

I accompanied her to her tent, then reluctantly walked back to the hotel.

The air in Hinsworth's room was dank and oppressive, with the cloying, sweet scent of medicine making me catch my breath. I hurried over to the window and opened it a few inches, letting in the salty night breeze.

There was one lamp, set so low it was hard to see. Hinsworth was nothing more than a long mound on the bed. He made no sound—I couldn't even hear him breathing.

I was tempted to leave. If he died in the night, it would be a cause for joy. The man was still under the influence of a powerful sedative, so I could smother him with a pillow. End his life. One life taken for the six lives he'd stolen and destroyed.

Something touched my hand.

I fumbled for the lamp at the bedside and raised the wick. The flame grew, and the room brightened.

Hinsworth was staring at me.

"Ana," he said, his voice thick. He blinked, as if he did not believe his own eyes.

I kept my distance. "Do you need water?"

He nodded. "Please."

His features were much changed, the hard edges gone.

I went to the dresser, poured a glass of water from the pitcher, then set it on the bedside table. Hanging back, I watched as Hinsworth struggled to sit up, but he was too weak.

"Help me," he said.

What I wanted, more than anything, was to pick up the pitcher and bring it crashing down onto his head. I'd promised Ewa I'd watch him, but doing so was more difficult than I had imagined.

I went over to him cautiously, as if approaching a dangerous animal, lifted his head, and tipped the glass against his lips. They were still red from the rouge he'd worn earlier that night. He drank greedily, one hand coming up to grasp my wrist to steady it. It was all I could do not to pull away.

His head fell back on the pillows, and he closed his eyes, a hand exploring his face. "Why am I sticky? Is it blood?"

My throat felt tight. It hurt to talk to the man. "It's just makeup."

He nodded but looked confused.

"You looked like a clown," I said. "Why did you want to look like a clown?"

He turned his face away, toward the window. "I don't know."

Hinsworth was quiet for so long, I thought he'd fallen back asleep. I was still standing, my back pressed against the wall.

"What happened to Silas?" he finally said. "Did I crush him when I fell?" His voice was tight, dripping with hope.

"I don't think so."

He groaned. When he turned to face me, he blinked slowly. "I'm not such a bad man, Ana. Your brother begged me to take you off his hands. Even offered to pay me. But I said no." He gave me a weak but lecherous smile. "That's got to count for something."

I laughed bitterly. "Are you expecting me to thank you? For that?"

"A little gratitude wouldn't hurt," he said petulantly.

My voice quivered when I spoke. "You have to undo what you've done to Javier and the others and set them free."

Hinsworth's expression hardened, and he snorted. "Javier's back in Mexico, where he probably found himself another pretty señorita." His eyes narrowed. "A señorita without the devil's mark on her back. But me? I kind of like it, if you know what I mean." He winked.

The rouge he'd smeared over his cheeks and lips stained the white pillowcase. It looked like blood.

I wished it were.

Chapter 25

Hinsworth dragged himself onto the stage the next night. His pain was etched into the deepening lines of his face, made up once again in that horrible white paint. The beasts were wheeled out again but remained behind the bars of their cage.

Ewa said Silas wasn't up to the stress of another show. Evidently, Friday's performance had nearly killed him.

Her words chilled me. I needed Silas to get well. With no other way to break the spell plaguing Javier, Silas was my only hope.

That night, I waited until I heard the gentle snores of the women before I slipped from my bed. Not bothering to change out of my long, white nightdress, I grabbed my thickest shawl, wrapped it around me, and pushed through the flap, into the fog descending upon the harbor. It swirled around me, obscuring my vision and muffling my footsteps. I had no lantern to light my way. Even if I had, I wouldn't have risked using it.

My heart raced. All I could see were the silhouetted shapes of boats bobbing in the water. I hurried past the saloon. For once, it was quiet, the men too tired to stay up drinking into the night.

I hurried toward a faint flicker of a light in the distance. Silas's cabin.

Wood shingles drooped and curled, giving the impression the building was molting. The cabin stood apart from the others. Cautiously, I walked around it, holding my breath, listening, but all was quiet.

If I knocked, Silas might tell me to go away. I tried the handle. It opened.

At first, I thought the room was empty. But then I saw him on the floor, nestled among a mound of blankets in a shadowy corner, books opened and scattered before him. A single lamp glowed on a low table covered in dirty plates and cups.

Silas registered no surprise at seeing me. "So, you've come," he said in his raspy, high voice.

Now that I was here, I didn't know what to say. A long, uneasy silence ensued. We stared at each other. Silas watched me warily, his head cocked to the side.

It was the first time I'd had such a long look at him. Silky golden curls cascaded around his face, illuminated by the soft light. With his cupid lips and pale complexion, he appeared angelic, yet something sinister lurked in his gray-eyed stare. My heart thundered, even though nothing bad had happened.

Yet.

"I've heard about you." His tone was plaintive.

"We talked through the door," I finally said. "On the ship."

He shifted in his nest. "And I told you to go away."

I glanced at the books. Words in a foreign language. Symbols I didn't recognize, strange diagrams. He leaned forward, body nearly toppling, and snapped the books shut. Dust motes rose into the air.

"Why are you here?" he demanded. His imperiousness reminded me of his brother.

Next to Silas was a wooden tray covered in objects: several small animal skulls, dried flowers, candles, vials, and a tarnished silver bell. An altar. My mother had kept one at home. Unlike hers, this one was not an offering to the Virgin de Guadelupe, but to something dark.

My heart raced faster, but I couldn't let fear get in my way. I took a deep breath and stepped forward.

"Silas." My voice was quaking. "I need your help. Whatever you did to Javier and the others, you need to undo it. Please."

Silas smiled, revealing a row of tiny white teeth. "Oh. And what is this Javier to you?"

"We were to be married," I whispered. "And then your brother took him."

Silas scowled. "That sounds like my brother. He takes what he wants. Does what he wants." He paused. "Has he taken you?"

I ignored his foul suggestion. "Please. Please, can you help? I won't tell your brother…or anyone."

"I can help you, but I require something in return." He paused, his words hanging heavy between us.

My skin prickled. "What?"

"I want to see your scar."

When I didn't say anything, Silas began to pout. "It's not fair. Everyone has seen it, except for me."

The room seemed to fall away, and I felt my chin tremble. Ever since I'd stepped foot on the *Iron Maiden*—no, before…since I'd left my family's hacienda—I'd felt powerless. Subject to the whims of a powerful man and his dark motives and vices.

Silas might appear outwardly childlike, but his body seemed to be coiled with a strange energy. Menace bubbled under that tragic exterior. If I refused, there was no telling how he would react.

"All right," I said, my voice dull.

Reaching under the shawl, I unbuttoned my blouse and dropped it to the floor, pulling the shawl to cover my chest. I turned around.

I could hear Silas's ragged breath behind me, but he said nothing. After a few moments, I snatched up my blouse and put it on. When I turned around, he was blinking rapidly, eyes overly bright.

"Are you a witch?" he asked, his voice shrill.

I considered his question for a long time before answering. "There are brujas and curanderas in my family," I lied. "Witches. Healers."

"It's the mark of the Devil himself," he whispered.

I'd heard that before.

Even from my own mother, unwilling to listen to the reassurances from the priest that it was nothing more than a scar. I suppose it was easier to believe in the devil than that her son was capable of such violence against his own sister.

"That's what people say," I replied calmly, lifting my chin. It wouldn't hurt for Silas, with whatever dark forces were at his disposal, to think I had some power of my own.

"Is it?" he demanded. "Did the Devil put it there?"

I thought of my brother, Nestor, and the evil on his face when he held my body down against the flames. I shrugged.

Silas was scowling now. "I don't sense your power. Are you hiding it from me?"

I shrugged again. "I've done what you've asked. We need to go to Javier now. As you promised."

Silas shook his head. "No. There's more." He paused, clearing his throat. "I want you to hold me."

My stomach flipped.

He snatched up a book and hurled it against a wall.

"It's not too much to ask, is it?" he cried. "My own mother didn't hold us, and ever since that damn surgeon took a knife to us, I've been alone. Cast aside. Ignored." He stopped, his thin shoulders drooping. "Please," he gasped. "Please hold me. I'll undo the spell. I swear it."

It wasn't his deformity making me uneasy. It wasn't the poor man's fault he'd come into this world missing his legs, cut from his brother by a surgeon's sharp knife. It was his disposition. His moods were so perverse and erratic, I couldn't help but feel afraid.

I didn't trust him any more than I could trust Hinsworth, but I had no choice. I had to try. For Javier.

Slowly, I went over to him and joined him on the blankets. He went perfectly still, the glisten of tears in his eyes. We had one thing in common. Both of us had brothers who had treated us with cruel disregard. Both of us had suffered at their hands.

I studied him for a moment, unsure how to manage what he asked. He licked his cupid lips and scooted toward me. I held my breath when his small hands circled my neck. Silas pulled himself onto my lap, his face inches away from mine. His breath had a musty odor, and I wondered if he was sick. His head nuzzled into my neck, and moments later, he pressed his warm lips on my skin.

"So beautiful," he whispered. He wriggled against me, pushing into my lap.

Bile filled my mouth.

It was too much. Without a word, I flipped him around so he was facing away from me, then I placed my arms around his chest. I would hold him, as he asked, but no more.

"I'm a man," he cried a moment later. "There is no tenderness in you."

"Be still," I said, sternly. With one hand, I began to stroke his forehead, like he was a small child, or as I used to do with Javier after he'd had headaches from too much time in the sun.

Silas squirmed in my lap, trying to turn around, but I held firm, and after a few moments, his body relaxed. Eventually, he went limp.

"This is nice," he whispered.

"Don't talk."

My hope was that he'd fall asleep, that ten minutes of ministrations would be enough to keep my end of the bargain. When I paused, he would make a pathetic mewling sound, and I would begin again. Several times, I had to slap away his hands as they explored the folds of my skirt. Eventually, he fell asleep.

It was still dark out, but the squawking of the gulls and the distant sound of men's voices suggested morning was not far off. We were running out of time. I jostled him awake.

He stirred. Reaching up a hand, Silas stroked my hair.

I shoved him off my lap and scrambled to my feet. He toppled sideways, glaring up at me.

"I've done what you asked," I wheezed, my fists clenching. "It's time for you to help me."

Silas shook his head, his lips tightly pressed together. His soft, delicate features hardened to cold marble. The realization he'd manipulated me made my throat go so tight I couldn't catch my breath.

"I won't," he roared, gray eyes glinting with rage.

Something inside me broke.

Yes, you will.

I spotted a length of rope dangling from a hook near the door.

With buzzing in my ears and the flesh of my scar burning, I snatched a blanket from the floor and threw it over Silas's head, securing it in place with the rope and tying the knot in back where he could not reach it. He was so caught off guard by my sudden movements, he hardly resisted.

I crossed the room to the leather harness Hinsworth had used to carry his brother, then tried to strap him into the contraption, but I could not get his arms through the openings with the blanket covering his head and torso. This presented a complication. Hinsworth said Silas had to see to use his powers, so I needed to cover his eyes. But in order to fit him into the harness, I'd have to remove the blanket and get his arms through the straps. I looked around. In the tiny kitchen, I spotted a stack of cloths used for cleaning and found one long enough to work.

Silas thrashed around wildly. It didn't matter. I was stronger, and if I could keep him from seeing me, I was safe. That gave me the courage to wrangle him into a position between my knees, whip away the blanket, and tie the cloth around his head, covering his eyes. The knot was so tight he screamed, his sharp nails scratching my hands.

My skin stung and began to bleed, but I ignored the pain and wrestled his wriggling body into the harness.

With Silas thrashing around, the task seemed to take forever. It would be light soon. I needed to get to Javier under the cover of darkness.

I realized what I was doing was madness, but I had no plan, only rage. My temper had run away with me, and I was powerless against it.

I secured the harness around my waist and stumbled out of the cabin.

After no more than half a dozen steps, Silas slammed the back of his head into my mouth. I was reeling when I heard a dreadful sound, and the ground rolled beneath my feet.

Chapter 26

At first, I thought Silas had found a way to make the earth move, to stop me from reaching the warehouse with Javier and the others. But as the ground continued its violent shaking, Silas shrieked in terror. I fell to my knees, understanding it wasn't his powers at work, but an earthquake. An earthquake more violent and powerful than any I'd experienced in San Sebastián.

Behind me, people emerged from their cabins, shouting. The shaking seemed to go on forever. When it finally stopped, I struggled to my feet.

I needed to get to the warehouse before anyone else did.

How I would make Silas do my bidding and reverse his magic, I did not know, but I had to get him there. I was on a mad quest, driven by anger and grief. Not even an earthquake would be enough to stop me.

As I drew closer, another vibration began beneath my feet, but I kept walking. Silas alternated between moaning and knocking his head into my chin. The iron taste of blood bloomed in my mouth. I pinched the little cabron, hard. He cried out in pain but stopped.

As I drew closer to the warehouse, the beasts howled from within.

"They're loose in there," Silas cried.

My blood went cold.

Did I dare enter the building if they had escaped their cages? Would Javier recognize me in his transformed state? Would he hurt me?

I didn't move, paralyzed by indecision, gripped by fear of the man I loved.

Gray light began to lighten the eastern sky, and I could see a figure running toward us on the dirt road.

It was Hinsworth. Yellow hair disheveled, white shirt unbuttoned, barefoot. Panic sent icy fingers racing up my arms. I looked around, but there was nowhere to run.

When he saw me, he stopped, mouth falling open, and stared at me for what felt like an eternity, confusion on his face. His eyebrows lowered when he registered the covered bundle strapped to my chest. I watched, heart pounding, as his expression shifted to shock, then anger.

"What are you doing, woman?" he thundered.

I opened my mouth, but no words would come out.

It was all written on his face. The wounded outrage of betrayal. The realization I had taken his brother. That I still wanted Javier.

The intensity and coldness of his stare froze my blood. I wanted to cry.

Silas tugged helplessly at the cloth covering his eyes. "My brother," he cried out. "The beasts."

Hinsworth ignored him, advancing toward me, hands balled into fists at his side.

"I said, what are you doing, Ana?" he bellowed.

Only Javier ever called me Ana. That those noxious lips would only utter half my name, the part reserved for another man, reawakened my fury.

"My name is Ana Maria!" I screamed.

Jack and two men I recognized as the beasts' handlers were racing for the warehouse. The shrieks and wails of the creatures filled the chilly morning air, but it was Hinsworth and his murderous expression that had my full attention.

In moments, he was standing in front of me, his chest pressed against his brother, reaching a hand around the back of my neck and squeezing.

"You're hurting me," I cried.

Hinsworth pressed his lips against my forehead, his teeth scraping my skin. "You haven't begun to hurt," he snarled.

Silas, smashed between us, cried out in protest. "The beasts, Ambrose."

The ground pushed against my feet. Hinsworth's eyes snapped open, his hand releasing its painful grip. He planted his legs wide, trying to steady himself as the earth bucked, then rolled.

With Silas strapped to my chest, I couldn't run. And I couldn't get past Hinsworth to the warehouse.

Why had I gone to Silas? It had been a foolish mission born of desperation, and now I was trapped. Defeat slumped my shoulders and muddled my thoughts. I could see no way out. Even if I did escape Hinsworth, where would I go? Devil's Landing was in the middle of nowhere.

The beasts roared, a sound that chilled my bones.

I looked over and saw the state of the building. Hinsworth did too, and his face paled. The low wooden structure listed to the side, sucked into a giant hole appearing beneath it. The windows had shattered. A furry hand appeared on a ledge, and a round dark head emerged, then a set of yellow eyes. The beast slithered out. Another followed.

"Dear God," Hinsworth muttered.

The first beast stood, its head cocked, attention fixed on the closest person. Jack. Two other men cowered behind him.

The creatures looked angry and hungry. Their bared, sharp teeth were terrible to behold. Even through the brine-scented air, their stink wafted toward me—the smell of wet, dirty animals. I couldn't tell which one had been Javier, and I choked back a sob.

All six of the beasts were out now, shuffling and snarling.

Hinsworth was transfixed.

I fumbled with the straps, desperately trying to loosen them and release Silas.

Jack yelled.

I dropped the harness and Silas with it. The bundle hit the ground with a dull, sickening thud. Hinsworth didn't notice his brother, still blindfolded, thrashing as if possessed by a demon. He didn't seem to hear Silas calling his name. *Ambrose. Ambrose. Ambrose.*

One of the beasts grabbed the strongman and threw him against the wall of the collapsing building with spine-cracking force. Jack toppled sideways, his screams mingling with the shrieking of the creatures, while another beast tore at Jack's chest with its claws. A splatter of blood. Jack writhed against the wall and then went still. Another beast straddled him, tearing at his chest and stomach, finally holding up a trophy of red, glistening organs.

A handler turned and ran toward the water, pursued by two monsters. One splash. Two. Three.

The other handler waved a long iron rod. I watched him swing it toward an advancing beast, but the creature dodged it. A second swing aimed higher and missed again, this time by only inches.

Silas had managed to remove the blindfold. He had propped himself into an upright position and was staring intensely at the chaos, lips moving.

When I looked back toward the collapsed building, it was just in time to watch a creature release its pent-up rage on a handler, ripping open his face with a powerful claw, then impaling him on the broken shards of glass protruding from the window.

Fishermen were charging up, brandishing long poles. I recognized some of their faces from my short time at Devil's Landing. The creatures that had chased a man into the water were hauling themselves up and over the side of the dock, their faces ferocious and savage, fur glistening. Hinsworth crouched over Silas, struggling to free him from the harness.

The ensuing melee was a cacophony of snarls, howls, and shouts of defiance, flashes of fur and steel.

When I realized with an icy shock that the carnage was just beginning, I fled.

Chapter 27

"You can't run away from me, Ana Maria!" Hinsworth thundered.

I'd made it as far as the dirt patch where the farmers' wives sold their goods. It was empty but far from quiet. Word had spread that the circus beasts were on the loose. Fishermen called to each other, shouting warnings. Men who had horses mounted them and galloped away from the chaos. Men with boats scrambled to push them off the docks, eager to escape the danger lurking on land.

Fear coiled in my stomach.

I spun around wildly, trying to decide where to go, when a familiar voice called out my name.

Hinsworth strode toward me, menace in every step. His shirt was patchy with blood, and a limp hobbled his gait. His lips were pinched tightly in a grimace of pain.

My heart dropped to my stomach, as heavy as a lava stone. "You're alive," I sputtered. "How?"

"Silas managed to fend them off." His breath was ragged and labored. He wriggled his fingers in the air before his hands dropped to his sides and he sagged with exhaustion.

"You left him behind?" I asked.

He lunged forward with an accusing finger directed at me. "*You* did."

I shivered. If I could have thrown Silas to the beasts like a scrap of meat to a crocodile, I would have done so without remorse.

"He's *your* brother," I reminded him.

Hinsworth let out a cold laugh. "Oh, Ana, you know all about troublesome brothers. Nothing seems to kill mine. I'm hoping the beasts will take care of him for me." He jerked his thumb over his shoulder. "Silas's magic isn't worth keeping him around anymore. It's done me more harm than good."

I gave an absent nod, mind racing, panic clawing at my throat, like Silas's sharp nails.

The beasts were loose and on a rampage. I was wasting time, standing there talking to a deranged man, when I needed to keep moving. Backing up a few steps, I was preparing to flee, when a tall figure appeared in the distance behind him. It was a fisherman, carrying Silas in his arms.

"Don't leave me brother," Silas cried. Dirt and tears streaked his porcelain cheeks. Golden curls fell over his eyes.

Hinsworth's mouth dropped open, and he spun around. "Will I never be rid of you?" he bellowed. His back was to me. His shirt was ripped, shredded in places.

The fisherman was tall and bony, with a bushy black beard. He stopped, a scowl coming to his weathered face.

"Is this not your brother?" the man demanded. His voice was deeper than Hinsworth's.

Silas stretched out his arms, as a baby might, reaching for his mother.

Hinsworth backed away, a look of disgust on his face.

The fisherman frowned and set Silas down on the ground. "I'm going home to my wife and away from all this madness."

Hinsworth glared at Silas. "This is all your fault. You went too far with the beasts. I told you to make them animals, not monsters. And now look at what you've done!"

Silas shook his head. "No. No. That's not what happened. It was a mistake. I tried…something new."

"New is not what I asked for, brother," Hinsworth yelled. He seemed to have forgotten all about me. With one final look of revulsion at Silas, he stormed off.

Silas glanced over at me, a scowl coming to his face. "You left me back there to die!"

I reacted in an explosion of fury.

"You should have," I screamed. "For what you did to those good men! Their lives were already hard enough, but they had people who loved them. Parents. Sisters. Brothers. Some even had children. You stole their lives, and for what? A stupid circus."

Silas placed his small hands over his cherubic face. "It's not my fault. Ambrose made me. He always makes me do things I don't want to do."

I wanted to take off my shawl, wrap it around him, and hurl the bundle into the water.

Silas dropped his hands and reached one toward me. "Look at me, Ana Maria. Do I look like I have many choices? Have pity on me. Please."

Clapping my hands over my ears, I demanded the liar shut up. "I've had enough of your mentiras. Cállate!"

Silas flinched, and his eyes bulged.

Something hissed behind me. In a flash, a dark figure ran past and crouched, wet and dripping, over Silas. There was a flurry of motion. Then Silas was silent and sprawled face-up. One small hand flopped in the dirt, the twitching caused by the beast gnawing at his chest.

My insides lurched at the sight of Silas's mangled body and the sound of the ravenous creature ripping him apart. I couldn't stay there, frozen in fear. When the beast was done, it would turn its attention to me.

I took a deep breath and slowly started to back away. At a corner, I bolted down the road, never looking back.

Chapter 28

The tent I shared with the other women was empty. I wondered where Ewa, Frieda, and the others had gone. I was suddenly exhausted, but I didn't dare rest. The tent was made of canvas and provided no protection.

Not knowing what else to do or where to go, I staggered outside.

The rising sun shone brightly that morning, strangely warm for a place usually shrouded in fog. The beauty of the day was at odds with the violent earthquake and the beasts' attacks.

Smoke drifted from a fire burning at the far end of the harbor, mingling with the salty scent of the sea. The seagulls had resumed their screeching.

It occurred to me the women might have gone to the hotel, so I headed there. I imagined myself renting a room on the third floor and barricading myself inside, pulling a dresser in front of the door, then lying down on the bed and taking a nap. I was so, so tired.

The saloon was still standing, and a man holding a rifle leaned against the railing.

"Liam's been looking all over for you," he called.

I waved but didn't reply, too eager to reach the hotel. It seemed the safest place to be.

After rounding another corner, I spotted Hinsworth. He was standing in the dirt lot between the post office and the whaling company building, clutching the sides of his head, looking around, mumbling.

The blood in my veins began to surge again.

I looked around but didn't see anything.

Hinsworth's face was flushed red, and the thin fabric of his bloodied shirt stuck to his chest. He was acting so strangely. Had he given into madness?

He caught sight of me and spun around, his eyes going wide. Then he shook his head.

"It's not safe," he hissed. "They're here. I know it."

Fear was like a noose tightening around my neck. I swiveled around, a hand pressed against my mouth, and scanned my surroundings. But I could see nothing.

"Leave," he said, his voice a hoarse whisper.

A shadow fell across the ground, and I looked up.

A beast stared down at us from the roof of the post office, its lips pulled back in a snarl.

Hinsworth looked up too. He gasped and took a few steps back, motioning for me to get away. In the full light of day, the creature was even more terrifying than it appeared in the misty gloom of the slough or the glow of the circus tent.

Hinsworth raised his arms into the air, fixing the beast with a steady gaze. His lips moved, and it seemed as if he were in a trance. It took me a moment to understand what he was doing. What Silas had done. Using his dark power to control them. Or trying to. But he had none.

The creature moved closer to the edge of the building, talons flashing in the sunlight.

Then it leapt, traversing the gap between it and Hinsworth as if it were no distance at all.

Hinsworth fell back with a scream, kicking. The creature howled, grabbed the man's ankle, and gave a mighty twist that sounded like the crack of a gunshot. Then it began slowly climbing up Hinsworth's legs, straddling him.

A yelp of terror escaped my lips when the beast raised a hand high above Hinsworth's chest, a red and yellow beaded ring on one finger.

The creature turned and stared, tensing, its limb frozen high in the air.

Before I could stop myself, I whispered his name. "Javier."

The creature blinked. Its mouth opened, revealing a ghastly row of teeth.

In its eyes, I saw a flash of recognition, and then it snarled. Hinsworth gave a high-pitched moan and a pleading look, as if I could save him.

The hand came down in a vicious swipe, tearing through Hinsworth's body. Skin ruptured. Bones splintered. Blood sprayed, dousing the wooden side of the post office in a splatter of crimson.

Chapter 29

I encountered Liam as I was walking along the outskirts of Devil's Landing. He ran up, put his jacket over my shoulders, and guided me to a bench in front of the saloon. The man with the rifle still stood guard out front, and he nodded when he saw us.

"I've been worried about you," Liam said, moving closer. "Do you know what's happened? The beasts broke free in the earthquake and have…attacked several men." He chose his words carefully so as not to frighten me.

I sighed. "I saw what happened."

"Are you all right?" He put an arm around my shoulders.

I nodded, pressing a hand against my eyes.

"None of the beasts were captured. Or killed. They went up the marsh, but they're still on the loose."

"I watched one take a boy from a farm on the slough," I said with a shudder.

Liam's green eyes widened. "You've seen some terrible things today, Miss."

"Yes," I whispered. "But I'm not the only one."

We sat in silence a while longer. I thought about my beautiful Javier, the evil of my brother and the Hinsworths that twisted him into a godless beast. And I thought of Javier's revenge.

Those creatures were born of tragedy, and tragedy would follow wherever they went.

Liam cleared his throat. "We should leave. We should go to Monterey. It will be safer there. Then we can decide what to do next."

"But I have no money."

He shook his head. "I have enough. Those things might come back, and we don't want to be around if they do."

We said goodbye to Ewa and Frieda. They looked past us, eyeing the slough nervously. Someone had placed a dirty tarp over the bodies.

"We're leaving as soon as we can," Ewa said. "Going to Los Angeles. Will you come with us?"

"No," I replied, and she didn't argue. We both knew why I had joined the circus. There was no longer any reason for me to stay.

I was too tired and too numb to consider the impropriety of traveling alone with Liam, a man I hardly knew. I only knew I could trust him.

By the time we arrived in Monterey, we were dead on our feet. Liam found cheap lodgings in a Chinese village at the north end of Cannery Row. It was a small inn run by the wife of a fisherman. I paid scant attention to the Chinese junks bobbing in the water, their design outlandish, their sails oddly shaped. The air smelled of drying fish, and our rooms were scented with incense.

The proprietress, noting our bedraggled state, gave us bowls of rice and squid.

We were assigned two rooms, but I was too afraid to be alone after everything that happened, so I asked Liam if he would stay in mine. He took some convincing, concerned about appearances, but he eventually relented and carried his cot into my room. No one objected.

"What do you think will happen to the beasts?" I asked, collapsing into the only chair in the room.

Liam stretched out on his cot and stared up at the ceiling. "I don't know. I don't see how something so fierce can ever be captured." He looked away, turning his face toward the wall. "Miss, can I ask you something?"

"Yes."

A heavy silence filled the room before he finally spoke again. "It was obvious Hinsworth fancied you. I never could understand why some of the ladies seemed to like him as well as they did. Did you…come to fancy him?"

I managed a weak laugh. "Never."

Liam let out a huge sigh. "I'm glad to hear it."

"Liam," I said. "Please stop calling me 'miss.' I'm Ana Maria. Just call me Ana."

He rolled over onto his side and propped himself up on an elbow. His green eyes regarded me solemnly. "All right, then. Ana it is."

Chapter 30

Frieda came to visit the next afternoon. The surviving members of the circus troupe were encamped in a dirt lot not far away, regrouping before heading south. With Hinsworth dead, Ewa had taken over. I was surprised Frieda had bothered to stop by.

"But how did you find us?" I asked.

Frieda sipped her tea and looked around, eyes wide with curiosity. We sat on the rough wooden steps to our room.

"Ewa divined it from her cards," Frieda replied.

"Impossible!"

She smiled. "I just happened to see Liam while I was taking a walk. He told me where to find you." Frieda was wearing a blue dress that matched her eyes, her thick gold hair piled high on top of her head.

"Do you have something to tell me?" I asked.

She shook her head and gave me an odd look. "No. I was just wondering how you were getting on, and if there was any chance you'd change your mind. About coming with us. I mean, you not knowing anybody."

But I barely knew them, I thought, but didn't say so.

Frieda cleared her throat and continued. "To tell you the truth, we could use your act. It was good. Real good. I know Ewa's sorry you're not staying on."

"I'm sure Louella and your sisters don't feel the same way."

Frieda burst out laughing. "No. No, they don't. They were jealous of you from the beginning. The silly cows. I always liked that you weren't the type to gossip." The smile disappeared. "And now I'll be stuck with them, without you around."

I stared at Frieda in disbelief. In the short time I'd known her, she'd accepted me as part of the troupe and done her best to include me, despite my resistance to her efforts. It occurred to me I hadn't been very kind to her.

The words escaped before I could think. "You...like me?" Then I winced—it sounded so pathetic.

Frieda laughed again. "Of course. I knew I liked you as soon as I saw you didn't go weak at the knees around HB. And I couldn't be more grateful for you cleaning up after us on the ship while we were sick. I just wished you would have given me a chance to get to know you better."

I nodded, suddenly feeling awkward with the turn in the conversation. It was time to change the subject.

"Did they catch the beasts?" I asked, then held my breath.

Her eyebrows lifted. "And who would be brave enough, or foolish enough, to do that? Those wild animals are vicious killers. They've fled up the slough, and the farmers' wives who live along the marsh are terrified, especially after what happened to that poor little boy. They want their husbands to hunt them down, but I think the men are too scared. They say they'd never find them because it's too wild up there at the end of the slough."

It made sense the creatures would escape to those densely wooded hills. When they were men, they'd come from the mountains above San Sebastián. My eyes felt hot and gummy. My plan to rescue Javier had failed. He would be, forever more, not the kind, handsome man I remembered, but a monster.

"I can't believe Hinsworth kept those horrible creatures on the ship with us," Frieda continued with a shudder. "What if they had escaped? They could have killed us all. And I still can't believe he let them out of the cage on opening night. But that was HB for you." She paused, looking down at her hands. "I do have something else to tell you. Jacopo died."

"Died?" I gasped. "The beasts?" That awful word. It would always trigger a deep ache of betrayal.

Frieda wiped a tear with the back of her hand and sniffed. "No. The earthquake. At the hotel. A chimney fell and broke through the roof. It crushed him in his bed."

"Que lastima," I whispered. And it was a pity.

It was nice spending time with Frieda, away from the bustle of the circus, and I found I didn't want her to go. "Would you like to take a walk down to the wharf?" I asked.

She nodded eagerly. While we ambled through the dusty streets, she hooked her arm through mine. At the pier, we bought fish sandwiches from an Italian man at a stall and ate them by the water, the breeze ruffling our hair while we watched the boats.

"Liam is nice," Frieda noted before we said goodbye. "He's always been sweet on you, you know."

I felt a flush creep up my neck and a flutter in my stomach. Liam had always been good to me, but I had never considered him in a romantic light. Mostly because I'd only ever loved Javier. But now, the Javier I'd known no longer existed, and for the first time in nearly fifteen years, I was alone.

We parted ways with a hug and some unexpected tears, but I couldn't shake what Frieda said. I decided to take a long walk next to the water, to clear my head before I returned to the inn…and to Liam.

Chapter 31

Liam and I stayed in our rooms in the Chinese village for a month. Captain Pendergrast secured a new ship and was again sailing the route from Mexico to San Francisco. He'd tried to persuade Liam to join his crew, but after dining with us one evening in Monterey and seeing us together, he relented. Instead, he put out word Liam was reliable and worked hard. With that recommendation, Liam had no trouble finding work with the fishing boats each morning.

In the evenings, Liam told me about his family in Ireland and his journey to England. He'd joined the *Iron Maiden's* crew on a whim. When I met him, he was already thinking of returning home.

"I missed the farm," he said. "And then..." His voice drifted off.

And then the shipwreck happened, and everything after that.

At first, I avoided his questions about my life in Mexico, but one evening he said, "What happened to your back?"

Maybe it was the red wine we'd had with dinner. The rough walls of our cabin seemed to fade away, and then I was twelve years old again, staring up at Nestor's twisted face, registering with shock the hatred in his eyes.

"My brother found me alone in our outdoor kitchen," I explained. "I was buttering a tortilla the cook made for me. When he found out I'd eaten the last one, he got so angry."

Liam leaned forward, resting his arms on the table. "Your brother? Your brother did that to you?"

"Yes."

The moment my brother's hands balled into fists, I'd known I was in trouble. Nestor had seized me by the wrist, yanking me away from the veranda where I stood and toward the large circular grill, with embers smoldering beneath it.

"I tried to pull away, but he was older and stronger," I explained. "He held me down so I couldn't move." I couldn't bring myself to say the rest. How Nestor leaned over me, leering with pleasure. How I felt my skin blistering from the heat.

Liam took my hand and squeezed it. "That's horrible."

I closed my eyes, remembering the unbearable pain, the smell of my burning flesh, my screams. "The cook saved me. Josefina. She was the only one who scared Nestor. She was carrying a broom. He let me go."

The relief I felt at finally sharing my story made my bones turn to jelly, and I was suddenly lightheaded. I couldn't tell Liam the rest. Not being from my country, he wouldn't understand.

It had been no secret my brother had always resented me, for being a girl when he'd wanted a brother and for my lighter complexion. Nestor had skin so dark the servants whispered he looked more like them than a member of the Carillo family. The boys at school were cruel about it, and so, in turn, Nestor was cruel to me.

He swore in front of the priest that I'd fallen on the grate, and he'd been trying to pull me up, that Josefina was lying because she'd never liked him. Nestor was half right. Josefina had taken against Nestor since she'd caught him swinging my kitten by its tail.

My mother stayed by my side while the doctor examined me. I lay on my stomach, biting on a wet rag, and he picked bits of singed fabric from my blistered skin. Josefina made a poultice of prickly pear cactus, egg yolks, and honey and applied it to the burn. She and my mother took turns staying by my side the rest of that night.

It took many weeks for my burn to heal, and as it did, I could see my scars reflected in my mother's face. Her expression of grim concern turned to disbelief and then, finally, to fear.

The priest came again. He patted my mother's hand, and later, he lit a candle, sprinkled holy water on my back, and muttered a prayer.

I wanted to scream at Father Gomez that it was Nestor who needed his prayers and not me.

My brother was never punished. Because he lied, swore even in front of Father Gomez, that I had fallen.

After my father died, I took over the accounts for our family's coffee farm. I tallied the number of days I'd spent in pain and, for each one, placed a peso in a box. And whenever Nestor slapped the raised flesh on my back, or struck me, or called me a whore, more pesos flowed into the box until I could no longer close it.

That was the money I'd taken to buy Javier's freedom.

Liam reached across the table and squeezed my hand. "And you had no one to defend you against that bastard of a brother?" he asked, green eyes widening.

I shook my head. When Javier had witnessed Nestor's abuse, his hands balled into fists, and his neck and face would go red. But as a worker on our farm, he was powerless against Nestor, a fact he'd learned when we were sixteen and he stepped between us. Nestor beat him so badly, he would have killed him if our father hadn't intervened.

"I don't suppose I'll ever meet him," Liam said darkly, "but if I did, he'd be sorry he ever touched you."

A warmth spread through my chest. His words, spoken with such fierce determination and conviction, made me smile. I thought of Nestor, bloated with drink and too much food, facing off against Liam, with the muscles he earned on the boats.

I looked around the cabin. A hovel, really. But it was clean and tidy, and with Liam around, I felt safe.

The next day, Liam had his first day off. Usually, he left to work on the boats long before sunrise, leaving the cabin to me. But that morning when I woke, he was already dressed, slicing bread and brewing tea.

"I have a surprise," he said over his shoulder.

I quickly pulled on a coat over my long nightdress. "Oh? What is it?"

Liam handed me a mug of tea, and I sipped it cautiously. It was black and strong, with a dash of cream. I longed for coffee, but it was too hard to make in our room.

"Then it wouldn't be a surprise," he said, grinning slyly. "But wear your nicest dress."

I only had three, and one I bought with money Liam had given me from his wages. At home, I had many clothes, some of them quite beautiful. Nestor had probably given them to one of his mistresses. I needed to find work, and soon. It wasn't right to accept money from this man. I wasn't anyone to him—not his responsibility.

Liam waited outside while I got ready. My hair was too straight to copy the popular style worn by Frieda, but I managed to pin some of it to the top of my head and let the rest hang down my back.

When I emerged in my green dress, the color of the parrots back home, Liam grinned.

"Where are we going?" I asked, unable to keep the excitement from my voice.

"You'll see." He took my arm.

We walked up many hills to reach our destination, and when I saw it, I gasped in wonder. The Hotel Del Monte spread before us, a vista of white buildings, red rooftops, and lush gardens. And above it all, a blue sky without a single cloud to block the sun.

Liam guided me through a maze made of hedges, past polo grounds, a racetrack, and a golf course. A stone bridge arched across a pond with lily pads. I was admiring the statuary when Liam tapped my arm.

"We're here."

Here took my breath away. I had to resist the urge to rub my eyes because, for a moment, I thought I was imagining things. That I was back home in Mexico. For the garden was filled with familiar plants: cactus, agaves, aloe, yuccas. There was even an enormous Saguaro. The sun warmed the top of my head, just as it had in the courtyard in San Sebastián.

"It's called the Arizona Garden," Liam explained. "The captain told me about it. He said the man who made it went to Mexico and brought all these plants back." He cleared his throat. "Do you like it?"

"Que hermoso!" I whispered.

The delighted look on his face made my heart swell.

Next to me, Liam shifted and tucked my hand into his elbow. My chest tightened. Time seemed to stop as my thoughts raced. This man was not Javier. I was betraying Javier's memory by the feelings I was developing for this Irishman.

I was caught between the urge to lean into the solidness of the living man next to me and to pull away out of loyalty to a man who was gone forever.

Hot tears stung my eyes, and I swallowed hard, hoping Liam wouldn't notice. But of course, he did.

"I'm glad I met you on that blasted ship," he said, pulling me closer, arms encircling my waist.

I couldn't resist. I leaned into his embrace, feeling the warmth and strength of his arms, not wanting to push him away. My hands came up around his neck, and then he was kissing me in the middle of the Arizona Garden.

When a group of young ladies began to giggle, I was too busy to care.

Chapter 32

As time passed and the horrors of Devil's Landing receded from my thoughts, I began to feel a longing for Los Peñas and the hacienda I had left behind. But I did not see how I could ever return. Nor could I stomach the idea of seeing Nestor again. My brother had scarred me and helped Hinsworth destroy the man I loved, and I was done with him.

I still thought of Javier—the man and the life that were lost to me. But in that fathomless void, my thoughts and my heart had turned firmly toward Liam.

We'd tired of living in such cramped quarters and looked at a tiny adobe to rent. When the landlord sternly asked if we were married, I felt my face go hot, but Liam did not lose his composure.

"That we are, sir," he replied quickly, managing to sound scandalized. "This is Mrs. Maguire."

My cheeks burned with embarrassment. After Liam paid the man a week's rent, I could hardly bring myself to look at him. We weren't living as man and wife, but our relationship was far from proper.

"Ana Maria Maguire has a nice ring to it, don't you think?" Liam asked, laughing.

He pronounced it "tink," and that brought a smile to my face.

He stopped, his face going red. "I did that badly, didn't I? I meant to ask, before we left, and then…"

Liam had started the morning more seriously than usual, saying we needed to have a talk, but then we got carried away with the demands of the day.

Seeing his stricken expression, I laughed, unable to help it. And then he was laughing too.

We were married that weekend before a Catholic priest. The man was tiny and bald…and too drunk to ask many questions.

Captain Pendergrast's journeys frequently brought him to Monterey, and we dined with him often. I suspected he was biding his time until he could try again to lure Liam onto his crew, but we became good friends, and he sometimes brought me news from Las Peñas.

It was on one such visit that the captain handed me an envelope written in a familiar hand.

My hands shook when I opened the letter, recognizing my uncle's handwriting. I felt an electric jolt as I read his words.

Nestor was dead. My brother had been killed when he'd fallen down the tile staircase at home, drunk.

My uncle continued on to say the estate now came to me, including the hacienda and the coffee farm. It was hard to believe Nestor was dead, even harder to believe I was now the sole owner of our business, free to do with it what I wanted.

We wanted.

Just that morning, Liam had been talking of returning to Ireland, having tired of working on boats. And while we had enough money for the passage across the ocean, we'd need to save more money to buy a plot of land.

Liam's gentle hand on my shoulder reminded me I was not alone. "Is everything all right?" he asked worriedly.

Both men stared at me expectantly.

"More than all right," I said, my voice shaky. "The coffee farm is ours."

Liam's green eyes lit up with a mixture of shock and delight. "Is this true?" He glanced over at the captain, as if he knew the answer.

I grabbed my husband's hand and kissed it. "We're going home," I said, my voice jubilant. "To Las Peñas."

Chapter 33

It had been several months since I'd last been on a ship, and while we were blessed with good weather and the captain's good company, I was still uneasy, waiting for an unexpected storm to blow in and dash us on the rocks.

This time, I was allowed to stay above deck in the fresh air as much as I wished. Liam never left my side, always holding my hand and sometimes holding a bucket in front of my face. Not because I was seasick, but because of my condition.

When the baby had made itself known, Liam said we should put off the journey, that it might not be safe to sail while with child. But I didn't feel safe in Monterey. Between earthquakes and terrifying beasts, I was ready to go.

Home. We were going home. To Mexico.

"I'll be happy to be back on a farm again," Liam said, his arm around my waist as we stared at the endless blue water. "But I know nothing about coffee."

"I'll teach you," I said.

"Is there anything you don't know?" Lian laughed and pulled me closer. "Accounting. Record keeping. Coffee beans."

"Babies," I said nervously. "I don't really know much about them."

The only babies I'd been around belonged to the servants, and I'd had little to do with them.

When the port of Las Peñas came into view—buildings white in the sun, the green of palm trees and hills rising into the blue sky—my heart swelled.

My return was bittersweet. I was coming home with a new husband and a new life in my belly, but it was a very different existence from the one I'd expected to have. I'd left Javier behind in a foreign land.

After our journey on horseback to San Sebastián, I gave Liam a tour of the hacienda. We went from room to room, Liam's mouth open the entire time as he took in the size of the place, the beauty of the courtyards, the lush gardens, and the servants.

He grinned and whistled. "What were you thinking when you left all this behind?" Then the smile vanished. He remembered Javier, and the memory made him uneasy. Only time and my love would reassure him.

I was struggling to make my own peace with my return. Everywhere I looked reminded me of Javier. The stables where he'd helped me on my horse. The roastery where he'd fixed the machines. His old room near the stables. But I was determined not to let those memories consume me. Javier was gone. I had a husband I loved, one made of flesh and blood, with ambition to grow our business.

As we walked through the kitchen, nibbling freshly made tortillas, he stopped and stared at the grate over the fire.

"Is that where it happened?" he asked.

I nodded and tried to pull him past it, but he wouldn't budge.

"There are two kitchens," he said. "Let's get rid of this thing. I don't like you looking at it, and I don't like looking at it either." He shook his head, frowning. "What a thing to keep around."

The next day, Liam accompanied me into the hills, where we found Javier's parents. They seemed to have shrunk since I'd last seen them, their faces etched with grief. I confirmed the rumors. Javier and the others had been kidnapped.

"They drowned in the shipwreck," I lied.

They heard the news, mute with grief.

I gave them money. Nothing would ever compensate them for the loss of their son, but it was the only thing I could think of. We visited the wives and parents of the other men and gave them the sad news, money too.

The next morning, we called together all of the workers from the farm and the hacienda.

"You'll be paid once a week," I promised them. "And more than you were making before. It will take some time to get the farm producing like it should, but once it is, we'll be able to pay you even better wages, so I hope you stay. And the land between here and the coffee fields we're going to split between you so you can farm it how you like."

That evening after dinner, we sat in the courtyard, throwing corn at the chachalacas. Liam was eager to explore the fields in the morning. I had plenty of work to do. Months' worth of receipts and papers to go through. But for that moment, I was just content to sit there, Liam's hand resting on my belly.

We didn't see Captain Pendergrast as often, as the journey from Las Peñas to San Sebastián was a long one. But when he came to visit a few years later, he told us of newspaper accounts of strange sightings, slaughtered farm animals, and a young woman found dead and bloodied on the foggy banks of the slough.

"The Slough Devil," the captain said with a shudder. "That's what they're calling it. But we know there are more than one."

My life in the circus seemed long ago…and Devil's Landing far away. But that night, and forever onward, the man I had once loved haunted my dreams, cursed to roam that lonely stretch of dark, shallow water.

The End

Keep Reading for a Preview of

Forest. Fungi. Family Secrets.

Chapter 1

March 2007

A cold, biting wind swept across the ravaged forest. David Eager stood at the edge of his land, surveying the chaos wrought by the merciless storm. He couldn't help but marvel at his property having been spared.

Surrounded by the ruins of Nils Forest, the Mendocino Wellness Haven cabins remained undisturbed. The vast expanse of trees had served as a barrier against the violent gusts coming down from the mountain, reducing the edges of the old woodland to a tangled mess of shattered trunks and branches.

A freak storm—that's what the forest ranger had called it on the news.

It struck at 7:30 a.m., when he'd been alone in his house. The last guest had checked out the day before, and the next group wasn't due until the weekend. David had cowered in bed for minutes, listening to the howling wind, convinced he'd been imagining the ruckus.

He'd been imagining lots of things lately.

Something hard had slammed against the outside wall of the bedroom, jolting him into action. He'd mustered up the courage to look out the window. Through the early morning light, debris and foliage hurtled past, like a scene out of *The Wizard of Oz*.

It had taken a whole day for the laborers to clean up.

From the wide porch of his stone house, he watched his men going about their work, shaking their heads in disbelief at the untouched grape vines.

David made no effort to help. In the past, he would have joined in, trying to prove he was just a regular guy. But he *wasn't* a regular guy anymore. His once confident strides had shortened to a series of clumsy, unsteady steps. Despite all the tests, doctors were unable to diagnose his growing list of symptoms. But what concerned him the most was what was happening to his mind.

Anxiety twisted in his stomach like a snake. The destruction in the forest was almost a metaphor for his body. The ranger had said the forest would heal itself with time. It had recovered from worse—wildfires, diseases, invasive species, and pests. But he was no forest. His body was damaged beyond repair.

David tensed at the sound of approaching footsteps. The Haven's manager wasn't due for another hour. David didn't turn around. Didn't want to find out he was imagining things again.

"Mr. Eager?" The voice belonged to a young woman. Hesitant. Tentative.

He turned slowly and coughed in surprise.

She was unconventional but stunning. A cascade of golden hair stood out against her smooth brown skin. Her dark eyes were captivating, and her prominent nose gave her a strong, distinctive look.

The wind seemed to grow louder behind him, almost overpowering his voice when he introduced himself. "I'm David Eager."

The stranger couldn't be a guest. The retreat, known for providing a peaceful escape for overworked tech executives, catered to an older crowd.

She smiled, revealing a set of perfect white teeth. "I'm Maria Hart. Radio reporter from San Francisco. I was hoping—"

"That's a long way to come for nothing," he interrupted. "I don't give interviews. If you'd done your homework, you would have saved yourself the drive." His hands twitched with irritation, or maybe something more sinister.

"I know. That's what I tried to tell my boss, but he insisted on sending me anyway." She sighed. "I'm sorry about this. I'm new at the station, and I'm still trying to prove myself. If you would just give me a few minutes of your time, I'd really appreciate it."

Her frankness caught him off guard. The wind whipped Maria's hair across her face, and he noticed a mole above her upper lip. In the past, her youth and beauty might have tempted him. But now, those feelings had gone—another sign of his pathetic decline. Not that David had a chance. She didn't even look thirty, and he was pushing sixty.

Her dark eyes were pleading. "Please. Just five minutes, and I'll be out of here."

David couldn't think of an excuse. Time was no longer of the essence. He had five minutes. Hell, he had the rest of the day. He could stick to his principles and say, "I never talk to reporters." Which was true. Ever since his early days as an entrepreneur seeking investors for his startup, he had avoided speaking to the media.

Until now.

Maria Hart had cornered him, and he found himself giving in to her charming persistence.

"What did you want to talk about?"

Her lips relaxed into a smile. "Nothing controversial. I'm just curious about what led you to sell your company and why you decided to open this place. Can we go inside?"

David's gaze lowered, focusing on the ground. How could he make it to the house without Maria noticing his awkward gait? He would have to concentrate. Take careful steps. With luck, she'd be too busy congratulating herself on her exclusive story to notice the peculiar way he walked.

He needn't have worried. Maria left to retrieve her audio equipment from the car, which gave him enough time to reach the porch unnoticed. When she asked to use the bathroom, he pointed her toward the end of the hallway, hoping she wouldn't wander into his personal space. He didn't like the idea of her seeing his unmade bed with its rumpled sheets.

Outside, the trees swayed in the wind. Inside, Maria was talking. At first, he assumed she was on the phone, but soon after, the young reporter appeared, accompanied by his housekeeper. Anita was doing her best to hide her surprise at the presence of an unexpected guest.

"You want some coffee, Mr. David?" she asked.

"Yes, please, Anita. And some lunch would be nice. Maria's come all the way from San Francisco, so I'm guessing she might be hungry."

Maria perched on the chair next to him, a microphone cable draped across her lap. She flashed a smile at Anita. "That would be amazing, thank you. I'm starving, actually."

As promised, Maria only asked about his retirement—he was tired of working, plain and simple—and the retreat for overworked Silicon Valley executives—no one else had thought of opening one in Mendocino, close enough to drive but far enough to feel like a true getaway.

At his request, Anita served lunch on the porch. Maria ate her meal while wrapped in a green woolen blanket. Her gaze kept drifting to Nils Forest across the sun-drenched meadow. A massive pile of shattered branches and debris sat at the edge of the wide field, ready for the next truck to come and dispose of it all.

"Did you see the windstorm? The coverage looked unreal, like something out of an apocalypse movie."

David nodded. "That's the perfect description."

Maria sipped her coffee and frowned. "The station wants me to do a twofer."

"Oh?" David set down his mug.

"They also want me to cover the storm for a separate story. One of the scientists we talked to says these types of storms are going to become more common and more intense."

David sat back in his chair, stung. He'd flattered himself, fooled into thinking the radio station had sent the reporter all the way up here just for him, but he was merely an afterthought, a way for them to make the most of their trip. Grab a quick interview with the has-been recluse and get more bang for their gas money.

His time with Maria seemed to fly by. She was a rare listener, asking insightful questions. David found himself talking about the stress and exhaustion he'd faced, even telling her about a seizure he'd had ten years into his role as CEO.

"That's terrible," she murmured. Her sad eyes never left his face.

He shook his head. Picked a crumb off his flannel shirt. "I made myself sound so pathetic just now, didn't I?"

Maria plucked off her headphones. "No. You were just being honest. Your old job sounds terrible." She wrinkled her nose. "Some days, the stories I cover are so heartbreaking that I literally go home and cry. My roommate thinks I'm an idiot for becoming a reporter. She says I'm too sensitive. It's like someone who's afraid of blood choosing to be a surgeon."

"Sounds like you're an empath," David commented. He knew a thing or two about personality types—empaths were rare in Silicon Valley.

"That's what my therapist says."

David smiled. "I never thought I'd say this about meeting a journalist, but I've enjoyed our conversation."

David glanced at his phone and was surprised to see it was almost one o'clock. They had been chatting for almost two hours. Maria had one more story to cover, which included a ten-mile trip to the ranger station and who knew what else. It would be a draining day, followed by a long drive back to San Francisco on winding roads.

"Do you have a place to stay for the night?" he asked.

A look of annoyance crossed her face. "There's no budget for travel. I'll have to suck it up and cover a motel myself."

"What if you stayed here? In one of the cabins? They're vacant anyway. Anita can make you some dinner and leave it in the fridge for when you get back."

Maria sat up a little straighter, and she smiled. "Seriously? That would be amazing. Thank you so much! And that would give me time to explore the forest. I had no clue your place was right next to it, so it's super convenient." She pointed toward the trailhead. "Would you like to come with me and show me around? You must know it really well, and I'd love to get your perspective on the storm damage."

The thought of trying to keep up with this young, energetic woman filled him with trepidation. Just maneuvering around the flat paths on his property was already enough of a challenge.

"I really wish I could," he replied, his voice carrying a hint of regret, "but I have some things to take care of here, unfortunately."

Later, David watched Maria emerge from Cabin No. 6, dressed for hiking in a robin's-egg-blue jacket and boots, her hair pulled back in a ponytail. When she spotted him through the window, she waved, and he returned the gesture. She disappeared into the forest, her audio equipment bag slung over her shoulder.

After hours had passed and the sun began to slide behind the trees, Maria appeared at the door, panting as if she'd just finished a run. "You won't believe what I've found out there. It's incredible. The forest is covered in fungus. The ranger said the mycelium comes to help the forest recover."

"Mycelium?" David echoed, intrigued. He knew there were mushrooms in the forest, but he didn't know much about them.

"Yes, mycelium. They're these white roots that sprout from the fungus or something. At least, that's what I think he said. There are mats of them everywhere, and they're so dense they look like blankets. This is so cool because I've been wanting to cover more environmental stories, and this one is fascinating. I was devastated when I saw how many trees were knocked down. At first, I thought the white stuff was a disease, until the ranger explained what mycelium does. And while I was out there, I found some crazy-looking mushrooms, so I picked some to show to the ranger. And guess what they were?"

Her excitement was contagious, and David found himself smiling. "What?"

Maria's dark eyes glittered. "Magic mushrooms! The kind that makes people trip out. Or at least, that's what he thought." Maria glanced down at her phone. "I have to go. I'm meeting with a mushroom expert. He's going to explain everything to me. I'll see you later. When I'm done."

Maria turned on her heels and sprinted back toward the trailhead, feet pounding against the ground as she ran through the trees.

The forest seemed to swallow her whole.

More Books by Debra Castaneda

Dark Earth Rising

Themed novels that can be read in any order

The Spore Queen

A charming reporter, an ailing tech mogul, and two strangers hiding secrets are brought together by a mysterious fungus, one that will either save them or destroy them.

The Devil's Shallows

Eight miles of mystery. One night of terror. Residents trapped in a remote neighborhood confront the unimaginable.

The Copper Man

Haunted tunnels. Unexplained deaths. Eerie sightings. Decades after The Copper Man killed her brother, Leah Shaw returns to the remote mining town of Tribulation Gulch where a lethal mystery awaits.

The Root Witch

A beautiful forest. A terrifying legend. It's 1986. Two strangers, hundreds of miles apart, grapple with disturbing incidents in a one-of-a-kind quaking aspen forest.

A Dark and Rising Tide

When a massive storm surge hits the central coast of California, the ferocious surf destroys buildings, floods streets, and washes up something sinister from the depths of the Monterey Bay.

Chavez Ravine Novels

Stand-alone novels set in Chavez Ravine, Los Angeles during turbulent times

The Monsters of Chavez Ravine

A 2021 International Latino Book Awards Gold Medal Winner! Before Dodger Stadium, dark forces terrorized Chavez Ravine.

The Night Lady

A rebel curandera, a plucky seamstress, and a young reporter are pulled into the investigation of a killer terrorizing Chavez Ravine.

www.ingramcontent.com/pod-product-compliance
Lightning Source LLC
LaVergne TN
LVHW090519110826
845146LV00003B/915

* 9 7 9 8 9 8 7 7 4 6 9 4 3 *